SO-AHY-870

J   Hunter, Erin.
Hun   Breakers of the Code.

DATE DUE

East Moline Public Library
745 16th Avenue
East Moline IL 61244

THUNDER ON THE PLAINS

BRAVELANDS

BREAKERS OF
THE CODE

BRAVELANDS

Book One: *Broken Pride*
Book Two: *Code of Honor*
Book Three: *Blood and Bone*
Book Four: *Shifting Shadows*
Book Five: *The Spirit-Eaters*
Book Six: *Oathkeeper*

CURSE OF THE SANDTONGUE

Book One: *Shadows on the Mountain*
Book Two: *The Venom Spreads*
Book Three: *Blood on the Plains*

THUNDER ON THE PLAINS

Book One: *The Shattered Horn*
Book Two: *Breakers of the Code*

THUNDER ON THE PLAINS

BRAVELANDS

BREAKERS OF
THE CODE

ERIN
HUNTER

HARPER

An Imprint of HarperCollinsPublishers

Bravelands: Thunder on the Plains: Breakers of the Code
Copyright © 2024 by Working Partners Ltd
Series created by Working Partners Ltd
Map art © 2021 by Virginia Allyn
Interior art © 2021 by Owen Richardson
All rights reserved. Printed in the United States of America.
No part of this book may be used or reproduced in any manner
whatsoever without written permission except in the case of brief
quotations embodied in critical articles and reviews. For information
address HarperCollins Children's Books, a division of HarperCollins
Publishers, 195 Broadway, New York, NY 10007.
www.harpercollinschildrens.com

Library of Congress Control Number: 2023936925
ISBN 978-0-06-296700-8

Typography by Ellice M. Lee
23 24 25 26 27 LBC 5 4 3 2 1

First Edition

THUNDER ON THE PLAINS

BRAVELANDS

BREAKERS OF
THE CODE

Tangled Forest

BRAVELANDS

Cheetah's Hunting Grounds

Grandmother River

"Quaking" Plains

PROLOGUE

"It's perfect."

Stonehide couldn't help swaggering a little as he emerged from the tunnel. He pushed one shoulder against the loose earth as he did so, widening the entrance some more.

"Abandoned long ago, not a termite in sight. The central chamber's lovely, nice and big, sheltered but with a bit of sun from the holes in the mound. Superb stuff."

Silvertail let out a sigh of relief. "Well done, my love. I was hoping this would be the one. And there's room for all of us?" She looked pointedly down at the rounded sides of her belly.

"I promise." Stonehide chuckled. "We'll have plenty of space. All it needs is a good covering of leaves, and it'll be a bed fit for the Great Mother herself."

"Well, you'd better get going and gather some then." Silvertail grinned. "It won't be long now, and . . . you know, I

1

think there might be two of them in there."

"*Two?*" Stonehide's muzzle went slack.

Silvertail's jaws opened in a happy grin, showing off the sharpness of her teeth. "And if they're anything like their father, they'll be rowdy little beasts."

"All right. Leaves for four!" Stonehide muttered happily, heading for the closest patch of trees while Silvertail slowly sniffed her way around the perimeter of their new home.

Two cubs. Thank the Spirit we found this place in time!

He felt a small pang of homesickness for their old den, where he'd been born and his mother before him, and where he'd always imagined raising their cubs. But it was gone, flooded out in the big storm, and there was no sense in looking back. *Best paw forward!*

"Stonehide!" Silvertail's voice was shrill and startled, and he turned back and broke into a run even before she'd said, "I smell lions!"

He smelled them too. The wind had changed direction, and now the stink of big ugly predators was everywhere. And sure enough, the tawny fur and thin mane of a young lion emerged from behind the termite mound. Its jaws were open, scenting the air, a thin droplet of drool splashing onto the dry ground.

Fear and anger were always hard to tell apart. Despite the drop in his stomach, Stonehide saw red.

"Get inside!" he yelled to Silvertail, and he took a running leap at the lion's face. The big cat flinched, and Stonehide pressed his advantage, jumping up again and clawing wildly at the creature's muzzle. "Scram!" he yowled. Like his father had taught him. Most predators were cowards. Attack first, and it was often enough to see them off.

The lion let out a roar and swiped at Stonehide wildly with one paw. Stonehide felt the claws drag through his fur harmlessly, unable to penetrate. He was knocked over, but he rolled and came back in one smooth movement, screaming, his teeth bared. The lion's roar faltered as Stonehide sank them into its other foreleg. He didn't hold on tight, though he could have. Just a little nip—drawing a gout of blood, making the lion twitch and stumble—to show this upstart creature whose territory he stood on. This one was young. It probably hadn't met one of his kind before. *Most lions will mess with you only once*, his father had said, *if you teach them a lesson the first time*.

"No easy pickings here," Stonehide spat, the lion's blood warm on his muzzle. "Get lost!"

The lion backed away, limping. "What are you, anyway?" he gasped.

Just as he'd thought. A novice, plumped up with false confidence.

"I'm your worst nightmare." Stonehide grinned.

He lunged again—just a feint, but it did the job. The lion gave a startled cry and turned to flee, limping and looking over its shoulder to make sure he wasn't following.

Except . . . there was a look on the creature's face now that wasn't fear or confusion. It looked . . . smug. Humbled, but knowing.

Stonehide was already turning when he heard Silvertail's cry. It was achingly far away, among the trees where he'd been going to get bedding for their new home.

He was already running when he saw the blood at the mouth of the cave and the claw marks in the dirt, the trail leading to the trees. Just beyond them he could hear Silvertail hissing and spitting, screaming out furious curses.

It had been a trick. A distraction . . .

She was giving them a fight, that much was certain. Growls and her own defiant cries intermingled. If he could get to her, it would be all right. He'd fight until his last breath.

He was still several paces from the trees when the sounds stopped.

Silence filled the world. The distance seemed to stretch out endlessly in front of him, but inevitably he reached the trees and the sight of two lions spattered with blood. They each had deep scratches and bites on their legs, a coating of blood dripping from their muzzles as they looked up from the unmoving shape of Silvertail.

Stonehide's fur stood on end, and he dug his claws into the earth, his sides swelling as he took a breath, ready to scream and leap at the lions. He would drive his grief into their eyes with his claws. . . .

But three more lion shapes loomed behind these two. One much bigger and one small and scrawny, limping a little as it let out an evil chuckle.

"Easy pickings," the lion said.

1

Flicker's scent was dusky and sweet, like the wind in the grass when the pollen was rising. Stride's heart soared the moment he smelled it, before he had even opened his eyes. He rolled over, yawning and tasting the air. On his back, his belly exposed and paws tucked up playfully around his muzzle, he blinked open his eyes and gazed up at his mate.

Her eyes reflected the light of the stars overhead, and he felt the tickle of her breath as she leaned in and licked his ear.

"You are about the laziest cheetah I've ever met," she said.

"Yet somehow still the fastest," Stride boasted automatically.

"And the most arrogant."

That too, perhaps.

In reality, he knew that she matched him for speed. And perhaps there were other cheetahs, outside Bravelands, who could give him a fair race. But he wouldn't admit it. Who needed reality, anyway?

In reality . . .

Flicker's eyes were full of stars, but her pelt shifted and blurred. Her beautiful spots were faint, her colors muted.

"You're . . ." Stride swallowed the word *dead*. What if saying it aloud made it true all over again? "You're a spirit," he said instead.

She blinked, and when she did all the stars in the sky seemed to go out, just for a moment. "Yes," she said. "I will be with the stars soon. But I'll always be able to look down and see you."

"I want to come with you," Stride said, rolling to his paws. "I don't want to stay here alone."

Flicker pressed her forehead to his, the sensation soft and fuzzy but painfully real too.

"You will," she told him. "One day. There's no hurry, my love. Live first. *Live*, Stride. Run and hunt. You have time to find another mate."

"I don't want another mate."

She pulled away from him and began to walk away. The stars shone brighter through her fading pelt, and Stride's heart ached as if some great animal was crushing it in their jaws.

"Wait! I don't need anyone else. I want you."

Flicker's steps faltered, and for a moment Stride thought she was about to turn around and come back to him. But then he saw her stagger and felt the shaking of the earth beneath his own paws. She turned back to look at him, her starry eyes full of confusion and alarm, and then the ground cracked open ahead of her, falling away in a dusty cloud. From the splits, black tendrils snaked out, like smoke, or like a swarm of flies. As Flicker was still struggling for balance, they wrapped themselves around Flicker's legs, her neck, her tail, making her squirm and yowl in panic. Stride was already running over the trembling ground, but he stumbled, unable to keep his own paws under him.

"Stride?" she mumbled. She was straining, but the smoke seemed to cling to her, insubstantial yet powerful, like a grass-eater crossing a waterway, caught in the grip of an unseen crocodile.

With a cry of fear, Flicker was dragged down into the black abyss at her paws. He heard her call his name as he called hers.

And then she was gone, snatched by the darkness.

Stride woke with a jolt so violent that he was on his paws before he knew where he was, teeth bared, swaying and snarling at nothing.

"What?" grumbled a voice. It was Stonehide, the honey badger, beside him. "What's happening?"

The real world slowly came back into focus in front of Stride's nose: a tangle of twigs and vines, thirsty-looking in the long dry season, but still green. Thick tree roots, and the sounds and smells of forest creatures all around. Stonehide's beady eyes squinting up at him.

"Bad dream?" he asked, his tail thrashing in annoyance.

EAST MOLINE PUBLIC LIBRARY

"I don't . . . I don't know," Stride mumbled.

Was it a dream? It felt so real. So horrifying. What a dream to have out of nowhere! Stride stretched out his spine, letting his claws sink into the ground, trying to shake out the dread that still gripped his bunched muscles. It was like no dream he'd ever had before, and he wasn't ready to dismiss it. What if something bad was happening to Flicker's spirit right now? His paws felt restless, as if he could still run to her aid, but there was nowhere in the waking world his speed could take him that would help her.

He stepped away into the undergrowth.

"Where are you going?" asked the honey badger.

"I need to speak to the Great Mother," said Stride.

"About a dream?" asked his companion incredulously.

"For advice."

He didn't wait, but he was grateful to hear the small creature's paws following behind him, even if he did mutter under his breath about getting a good night's sleep.

If something really was wrong, the Great Mother would know what to do. At least he hoped so.

"I think when she has anything more to say, she'll come find you," Stonehide said coolly.

"No, this is . . . something else," Stride said. But was it? Horrible dreams, strange signs from the sky—it all felt like part of the same thing.

He'd never been a *visions* kind of cheetah before Flicker's death. That sort of thing happened to other animals, like elephants and vultures. But since his mate had fallen dead at his

EAST MOLINE PUBLIC LIBRARY

paws, killed by the shadow that chased every cheetah when they ran too fast, that had changed.

Flicker's sign had sent him to the Great Mother, and the elderly elephant had agreed that she thought he was here for a reason, even if she'd said Flicker's death had been natural. The Great Parent was supposed to know such things, and who was he to question it? It had been days now, living in the forest, where he couldn't stretch his legs or find prey bigger than a warthog, and Starlight, despite her assurances, had barely spoken to him.

"Well, whatever it is," Stonehide said, catching up to Stride as he negotiated a thicket of vines, "if the Spirit has answers, or a task for you, you'll know it soon enough."

Stride frowned and let out a low growl of frustration. "What kind of Spirit lets an innocent cheetah just *die* for no reason?" he muttered.

"The kind we've got," said Stonehide flatly. "Starlight told you. It was a good—a *natural* death. Nothing to be done. It's better if you start trying to accept that now."

"Thank you for the advice," grumbled Stride, "but that's not good enough! Not when I still feel her presence all the time! Not when . . . when I'm seeing things . . ." Stride trailed off with a strained yowl. Stonehide might be right. His dream might have been no more than a dream. "I'm trying. But we were *meant* to be together. How can I just *let her go?*"

Stonehide didn't seem to have a reply for that.

Though it was the early morning, plenty of animals already gathered around the Great Parent's clearing.

Legend said that the trees had once been muscled aside and torn up by elephants to make room for the animals to visit a baboon Great Father in his own forest. Ever since then, the steady stream of creatures tramping over—and eating—the undergrowth kept the space open and empty enough to accommodate several elephants and a crowd of smaller animals.

Right now, there was a rhino with a broken horn; a small herd of dik-diks chattering and wiggling their long noses at one another; a huge lizard with legs like tree roots; and a gang of small mammals who jostled and shoved to try to get as close to the Great Mother, and as far away from the lizard, as they could.

If Stride waited for Starlight to hear out all these creatures, he would be waiting all day. And what if Flicker didn't have that kind of time? If he closed his eyes, he could still hear her panicked voice as the black . . . *stuff* . . . enveloped her limbs.

He decided to push to the front. It was *important*. And the small mammals and the dik-diks could hardly stand up to him, and the lizard . . . well, the lizard didn't speak grass-tongue, so as long as he stayed out of snapping distance he could ignore it.

"Come on," he said to Stonehide, and started forward into the clearing.

He heard some muttering from the crowd and tried to ignore it. But then his ears swiveled as he heard a small, high voice gasp, "*Codebreaker!*"

I am no Codebreaker! he thought, and turned to see who had called him one. He spotted the creature, a monkey of some sort, with its paw protectively on the flank of a smaller one. But it wasn't looking at him. It was staring right at Stonehide.

Stride opened his mouth to tell the creatures that Stonehide wasn't a Codebreaker either—a dangerous beast for his size, yes, and grumpy along with it, but he killed only to survive, he wasn't a murderer—but then he caught the look in Stonehide's eyes as he quickly turned his face away from the two creatures.

It was shame.

Stride looked away too. He walked on a few paces with Stonehide on his tail, putting a little more space between the whispering animals and him. They drew close to the rhino, and Stride stopped, knowing that there was one creature who would not tolerate him pushing ahead of them to speak to the Great Mother.

"Stonehide," Stride said quietly. He drew breath to ask what the monkey had meant, but Stonehide cut him off.

"Mind your own business," the honey badger snapped.

Stride's fur bristled. "It is my business, if I've been traveling with a Codebreaker!" he hissed back.

Stonehide gave a snort. "I don't need this. You stay here and pester the elephant about your dead mate if you want, but you're wasting her time." And with that, he turned and skulked off, sending dik-diks scattering out of his way.

Stride stared after him, shock and confusion making his

tail twitch. What was all that about? If Stonehide was really a Codebreaker, why come with him to see the Great Parent in the first place?

Maybe there's more than one thing I need to ask the Great Mother about. . . .

2

The grasslands were alive with small noises: the wind in the dry leaves, the chirping and chattering of small animals, Bellow's labored breathing. But to Whisper, it felt eerily quiet.

It was *wrong,* in a way that rattled her heart in her chest, for any buffalo to be apart from their herd for this long. Not without some goal, some journey, and a return to the herd always in sight. Now the herd had left under the leadership of Bellow's scheming, usurping brother Holler. Only three of them had stayed behind: Bellow, with his terrible injury all but guaranteeing he would die if he tried to follow the migration; Whisper, who had seen Holler's treachery for what it was; and Thunder, her surrogate mother, whose own daughter Murmur had been killed by Holler's awful son, Quake.

Every other buffalo in the herd had decided that safety was more important than loyalty. Now that the comforting drumming of their hooves had faded into silence, Whisper could almost understand it. It wasn't too late to follow. To take comfort, if not solace, in the safety of numbers. Her head told her to move after them, but her heart remained rooted.

Bellow shifted again, limping to a slightly fresher patch of grass. His one magnificent curling horn gave him a lopsided look as he bent to try to eat, the other one broken off in the duel with Holler. It still lay a little way away, already giving shelter to a colony of ants.

Whisper and Thunder stood together under the shade of a tree, close enough to Bellow that they could run to his aid if he needed them, but far enough that he couldn't hear them if they kept their voices down.

"What can we do?" Whisper asked Thunder. She was a big, adult buffalo. She had always commanded the attention of all the most powerful males, and the other females had always listened to her—at least, until now. She must have some ideas. "If a pack of lions comes along, I don't think . . ." It hurt to say the words, to reduce the once-powerful Bellow to this, but she forced herself. "I don't think we can protect him."

There was a time not even the strongest or hungriest of lions would have messed with a buffalo like Bellow—he'd have shaken them off like flies, tossed them skyward with a flick of his horns, or crushed their skulls like eggs. Not anymore.

Thunder's expression was dark. "No. We can't."

"Well then? What do we *do*?" Whisper said again.

She looked at Bellow and suddenly felt as if she could see

the shape of another buffalo standing there, tiny in comparison to Bellow's massive bulk.

Echo.

She had always been so worried about her little brother falling behind or hurting himself or getting lost. But she hadn't been able to save him from Holler's betrayal. She tried to push the memories away, but she couldn't. His panicked squeal at the cliff edge, pressed back by hyenas until his hooves slipped over the edge. If only she had been closer, she might have saved him from the fall into the river far below. That he would've died quickly was hardly a comfort. He was so young. So innocent. And unlikely as it had seemed at the time, he had been chosen by the oxpeckers to lead the herd.

Fury blazed beneath her grief and guilt. Holler should have protected him. The hyenas should never have been allowed to get close.

"Perhaps . . . ," Thunder began, her voice shaking, and Whisper knew what she was about to suggest before she even said it. "Perhaps we did the wrong thing. Perhaps if we could persuade him to try to catch up with the herd . . ."

"No!" Whisper cried. "Even if he could, he's made his choice, and it was the right one!"

"I'm injured, not deaf," said Bellow. He limped toward them, his eyes gleaming. His intention was clearly to march over and interrupt their conversation, but his steps were so slow and faltering that Whisper and Thunder exchanged a look and then hurried over to him themselves.

"I know it's hard," Bellow panted. "It might be the end of me. But believe me, there is no safety in that herd. My brother is leading them to their dooms, and the doom of all Bravelands."

"It's true," Whisper said. "Remember, he doesn't know the Way!"

Thunder hung her head. "Bellow, I know he betrayed you, but . . . would it not have been better for us all if you had given him the ancient knowledge, as if he really was the leader?"

Bellow's eyes narrowed, and he raised his head. "I could not have done so, even if I felt inclined—which I do not," he sniffed. "No buffalo who behaves as Holler has can be trusted with the Way. What's more, the oxpeckers do not lie. They chose our new leader. They have not chosen another."

He nodded across the grass, to a place where the ground fell away into a deep valley, the same one where Echo had fallen to his death. Whisper shuddered as she saw that the trees along the edge of the cliff were crowded with small birds, most of them with vibrant orange beaks.

"But Bellow," Thunder said softly. "Echo is dead."

The words struck Whisper in the chest, stealing her breath for a moment.

He was my little brother, and I let him die.

Silence fell between them, awkward and heavy.

"Well. We cannot just stay here," Thunder said, tossing her head. "We need to find more to eat. I say let's head toward the sunrise; I saw clouds there this morning, there might have been some rain."

"I doubt it," Bellow said darkly, but he slowly nodded. "But you are right, Thunder—we must survive, or there will be no hope for our kind at all. Let us go."

They let Bellow take the lead, setting the slow pace as they pointed their horns toward the rising sun. Whisper looked back, just once, to the tree where the oxpeckers were still sitting. Their orange beaks were still, their voices silent, as if they were grieving too.

The sun had passed over their heads and their shadows were overtaking them when they crossed a small hillock, stopping at the top to graze on some windblown grasses. Whisper had just lowered her muzzle to the ground, when the ground suddenly spoke to her.

"Hey! Hey! Is it them again?"

"No, different ones!"

"What do you mean, different ones?"

"Three buffalo, big ones. No lions!"

"No lions?"

A moment later, a furry head popped out of a hole in the ground right in front of her face, little dark eyes glinting suspiciously. The meerkat sniffed the air, stared at her for a moment, and then called down to its colony.

"Just buffalo!"

"Then tell them to keep the noise down," one of the other meerkats shouted from the bottom of the hole. "The kits are sleeping!"

"They're sleeping!" came another squeaky shout.

EAST MOLINE PUBLIC LIBRARY

"Yeah, we're sleeping!" echoed an even smaller, even squeakier voice.

"I'm sorry," Whisper said, suppressing a chuckle. "We'll try to be quiet."

Another meerkat sprang up from the hole, and then a third near Thunder's front hooves.

"Are you looking for the other one?" asked one, scratching its ears.

"What do you mean?" asked Thunder. "Did you see the herd?"

"No, not the herd," said the meerkat.

"Not the herd!" echoed one of the others.

"The little one," said the first meerkat. "On its own, with the lions."

"... *with* lions?" Whisper said, feeling herself weirdly drawn into the meerkats' repetitive way of talking. "What do you mean? A buffalo calf? Was it being chased?"

"Chased? Chased?" The meerkat peered down into the hole it had emerged from, as if it was checking with the others. "No, not really. Not stalked. Followed. Like they were friends."

"They were fattening him up," put in a meerkat with one partly bitten-off ear, popping up above the den. "Letting him eat, getting all tasty to eat later!"

"No, no," said another, pushing the last one out of the way. "That's clever! Lions are stupid! Probably thought he *was* a lion!"

"Not that stupid," snarled the one with the injured ear.

EAST MOLINE PUBLIC LIBRARY

"But he was alive?" Whisper asked. Her heart was suddenly hammering. It wasn't Echo. It couldn't be Echo. She'd seen the distance he fell, over rocks and into the river. It would take a miracle to survive. But even so, if there was a buffalo calf out there alone and she didn't try to find him, what was the point of any of this?

The meerkats didn't seem to hear her.

"Little buffalo gets too big, it gets too big for eating!" another one pointed out huffily.

"Listen . . . ," Whisper said, but now the meerkats were in full flow, repeating and contradicting one another in their chattering voices.

"Come on, Whisper," said Thunder, approaching and nudging her softly on the shoulder. "There's nothing we can do about this calf—if it even exists," she added, with a skeptical glare at the arguing meerkats. "These little creatures are always getting their stories mixed up. All that repetition, things get garbled."

Whisper frowned. She took a deep breath, then reared up, gave her best bellow, and drummed her hooves hard on the dry ground. It made a satisfyingly loud rattling sound. The meerkats let out a chorus of shrieks, and most of them ducked down into their holes, covering their ears.

"Where did they go?" Whisper demanded. "Which way?"

As one, the meerkats pointed shaking paws across the plains. Most of them pointed toward a faint line of shimmering water in the distance, though one pointed the opposite way for a moment before rejoining the consensus.

Whisper sighed. It wasn't a great sign.

"Whisper," said Bellow. "I would counsel you against doing anything rash on the word of these creatures." There was a pause as Whisper dithered, staring at the river on the horizon.

"It's not Echo," Thunder added. "I know what you're thinking. I wish I could help my poor Murmur, but I can't. And if we go after those lions, with Bellow injured as he is, we will not be able to protect him."

Whisper felt a weight strangely lifted off her at Thunder's words.

"Then I'll go alone."

"Whisper!" said Bellow sharply. "I forbid it, it's not safe."

"It's not safe for that calf either," said Whisper. She tried to pull herself to her full height—still barely half of Thunder's. "I promise, I'm not deluding myself, I don't expect to find my brother. But if I go after them myself, I might be able to sneak up on them and just see what's going on. If the calf is dead, or gone, or I can't see a way to help it, I'll come back and find you. But I have to do this." She looked up at Bellow, meeting his watering eyes. "It's the right thing to do."

Bellow let out a low moan, but there was a good-humored look in his face as he shook his head. "Doing the right thing has not worked out too well for us recently. Remember this, little one—and do it anyway."

"I will," Whisper promised.

"Well, good luck, goodbye!" said the meerkat, and vanished into the hole once more. A chorus of chittering voices from below called back "Good luck!" and "She's mad!" in about equal numbers.

Thunder blew a long breath through her muzzle, making the hair on Whisper's nose ruffle, and gave her a soft lick across the ear. "Please be careful, dear one. We will be looking for you."

Whisper nodded, gave Thunder a gentle headbutt, and bowed respectfully to Bellow, then she turned and headed off at a quick trot before she could change her mind.

I'll do this for Echo, she told herself. *He's dead, but some other calf will get to live, if I can possibly help it.*

Yet despite her promise to Thunder, despite it all, she couldn't stop a spark of impossible hope from growing, deep in her heart.

The oxpeckers didn't pick a new leader, and nobody knows why.

What if they knew their first choice was still alive . . . ?

3

Breathstealer's paws and shoulders ached. Her jaws were still sticky with the drying lion blood. Her heart pounded in her chest. She wanted to stop and lick her wounds and revel in it all: adrenaline, victory, vindication. She needed water too.

But there was no time to rest. The strange white vulture that had appeared to her was leading her at a relentless pace, waiting just long enough on a rock or a tree branch for her to catch up, then flying again, just far enough for her to see where they were going next. Every so often, whenever doubt entered her heart, the bird would fix her with a red-eyed stare, and she would hear that voice again, the deep voice that seemed to come from the bones of the earth.

"Follow."

It made her shiver every time with fear, and with excitement.

The Great Devourer needs me.

All her life, she had seen visions, been given strange glimpses and riddles that pointed toward the future. The other hyenas had scoffed and shunned her for daring to suggest they came from the Great Devourer, from Death itself, but she had always known. And now she was hearing the voice of the Devourer, here in the waking world. If the clan could see her now . . .

They would not care.

Breathstealer shook her head, clearing a fog of emotion that threatened to cloud her vision.

After she had tried so hard to save them from their own foolishness, she had been expelled from her clan. They had stripped her of everything that made her a hyena, even the insulting name they'd given her. *Tailgrabber.* Well, Tailgrabber was dead now. Breathstealer had killed her, along with the lion who'd killed her sister's cub. She had taken her life into her own jaws, and in that moment, the white vulture had come to her. It had to mean *something. . . .*

They had left the hyenas' territory some way back. The vulture passed over dried streambeds that were once fast-flowing rivers, between rocky kopjes, and over a flat grassland that seemed to roll on forever. All of a sudden, a dark line of shadow that Breathstealer had taken for a rock formation was looming up in front of her, and it wasn't a cliff, but a forest. The vulture landed on a twisted branch, glaring down at her, then it swept off between the trees with a hoarse cry.

"Follow."

The world beneath the trees was shady and crowded compared to the open grassland outside. Small creatures that had taken shelter from the relentless sun hustled out of her way as she passed, and insects buzzed around her head. Here, despite the lingering dry months, there were still traces of green that grew thicker and brighter as she pushed farther in.

The ground began to slope beneath her paws, and then she realized the cool air wasn't only because of the relative darkness cast by of the thick canopy above. The dry earth gave way to soft, decaying leaves, and then to damp grass and mud. The eyes of snakes and lizards swiveled to track her progress. More and more insects hummed around her, and they seemed to be larger and fatter than those at the edge of the forest.

She sneezed and tossed her head as the tips of her ears caught on a thick, trailing cobweb, and looking up, she could see it was only the lowest dangling string of a thick and tangled web. One curious spider the size of her paw with bright yellow stripes on its thin legs came scuttling to see what had disturbed its sleep. There were many more in the webs, dark shapes moving slowly across the branches or sitting perfectly still, waiting for their prey to blunder past.

They seemed to take no notice of the white vulture, which sat just ahead on a rock, half-hidden by thick ferns. It waited until Breathstealer had almost reached it, then hopped to another rock, then to a branch, and then down onto a mossy hillock. The muddy ground beneath her grew even wetter, even stickier, and Breathstealer had to focus all her attention on picking her way through it and keeping the fleeting bird in sight. It didn't seem to be slowing to let her catch up anymore, despite its obvious wish for her to follow.

She began to feel out of breath, panting as she pushed on through the bog. Her tongue became cold almost at once, and there was a strange taste on the air, something foul and rotten. At first, she thought that there was rot-meat here somewhere, some unfortunate creature caught in the bog that had never escaped and not yet been eaten. But the smell grew stronger, and worse, until it made her head spin.

She came to the tree where the vulture had been, looked up, and did not see it.

Where is it? She spun on the spot, her head suddenly feeling light and her vision swimming. *Where am I?*

There were no sounds of insects now, or birds, or the wind in the trees. There was nothing but the scent of death and the sound of her own ragged breathing. She had no idea which way would lead her back out of the darkness.

With every breath, the noxious scent seemed to creep into her mind and confuse her, stealing away her sense of smell, of direction, even her vision—beyond a few strides away, the forest faded into a green-black fog that had not been there a moment before. The drooping leaves and ferns around her seemed to shift with strange moving shapes. . . .

And then in a moment the shapes lifted from the leaves. Locusts, hundreds of them, swarming into the air and toward Breathstealer with a buzzing sound that felt like it was vibrating between her ears.

"*I am glad you came, Breathstealer.*"

Not the vulture's voice. This was deeper. More rasping. Not of this world. It came from the insects, but not from them at the same time. It spoke from inside Breathstealer's own body, and from under her paws. Breathstealer's knees crumpled, and she fell to her haunches in the mud, gasping as the swarm surrounded her.

"Are you . . . who are you?" she managed to choke out.

"*You know,*" said the voice.

Breathstealer took the deepest breath she could and bowed her head. "Great Devourer," she whispered. "You honor me by bringing me here. By showing me your visions. I have tried to follow them the best I can. I am your servant, as are all hyenas."

"*You are a very special creature, Breathstealer, Tailgrabber, Cub. Not all your kind could bear my gifts as you do.*"

"I . . . I've tried," Breathstealer said. "I've tried so hard. But I don't always understand them. . . ." She knew she should shut up, not babble uncontrollably in front of the Devourer himself, not if she wanted to live another day, but she couldn't seem to stop herself. "I knew what it meant when I saw my mother killing the old leader . . . and when the hyenas walked blindly off the cliff . . . I think I understood what I had to do? But there are others . . . the buffalo on the dead plain, asking for my help. What did that mean? What was I supposed to do?"

There was a silence, and for an awful minute, though the insects were still swarming about her, Breathstealer thought that the Devourer had fled.

Idiot! She chided herself. *You can't pester a spirit to explain itself like that!*

But then the voice returned, and if anything, the deep-down rumble had an edge of amusement in it.

"*Do?*" it said. "*Supposed to do? Dear one. You were supposed to do nothing—only what you will. You need not act, unless you wish to. My insects know truths beyond time and flesh. They bring them to you as gifts only.*"

"Gifts?" Breathstealer murmured. *Those "gifts" have cost me my family, my friends—any friends I might have had. They cost me my clan. They nearly cost me my life.*

She managed not to say that aloud, but the Great Devourer seemed to sense her hesitation.

"*As I said. Few creatures are strong enough.*"

"Then I'm strong," she replied, and to her surprise, she did feel strong, even though her head was still swimming. "But I'm all alone."

"*This is the price, and the reward: the truth of things to come, the power to choose—the power over life and death. And I can give you more. I can make you the most powerful creature in all Bravelands.*"

Breathstealer felt as if the spirit's words had picked her up and gently shaken her, making her head spin and turning everything she knew on its head.

She could say, *Yes, please, I'll accept any gift you want to give me.* And she should, shouldn't she? It was *the Great Devourer*, the ultimate fate of every creature in Bravelands, whom hyenas had followed forever. If she couldn't trust Death himself, what could she trust? Why wouldn't she say yes?

EAST MOLINE PUBLIC LIBRARY

Why didn't she *want* to say yes? What was holding her back?

"I . . . I don't want to be alone," was all she could think to say.

"*Take my offer, and you can choose your family from any creature, living or dead,*" said the voice. "*They will all do your bidding.*"

Breathstealer blinked, tried to breathe slowly—it was hard to understand any of this, let alone with the noxious, head-spinning scent in her nose and the endless buzzing of the locusts in her ears. It was harder and harder to hear her own thoughts, and they seemed to narrow down until all she could think was: *Why?*

"Why me?" she choked. "Why now? Why?"

"*The visions are our gift to you,*" the Devourer said softly. "*But there is a great wrong to be righted in Bravelands. Something was stolen, long ago. It is time to set things right.*"

That sounded good. It made sense. Obviously the Devourer needed something, and she would be happy to give it. She only wondered why it had been so reluctant to tell her before. Breathstealer began to relax, and a sleepiness crept over her. Standing in this mud, talking with Death, was *tiring*!

"Oh, dear. Does the Great Mother know? Should someone tell her?" she murmured.

The sound that came from all around her was terrifying, like the shriek of a dying animal. It snapped her out of her lethargy and made her cower, her chest fur dragging in the mud.

"*Do not mention that name here!*" the Great Devourer boomed. Breathstealer's fur rippled, alarm thrilling through

EAST MOLINE PUBLIC LIBRARY

her—not just at the horrible sound but at the words. She felt as if she had been dozing and had woken up with the scent of lions on the air.

"Why not?" she whispered. "The Gr—it—it's not your enemy. Right?"

"*Do you accept our offer or not?*" The locusts buzzed angrily.

Something is wrong here, very wrong. Self-preservation kicked at Breathstealer like an angry zebra. *Get out! Run!*

"I need to think about it," she gasped, and tried to pull her paws from the mud.

"*Perhaps you do not truly understand the power we are offering,*" said the Great Devourer, in a voice like mountains crumbling. "*You need to learn. Then you will understand.*"

The locusts broke apart, then swept over her like a wave, covering her with their battering wings. The voice was gone, the air suddenly colder than before. She yelped and staggered backward, but there was no *away*—the cloud was all around her, and she had no idea which way she'd come from. She started to feel small, sharp bites on her ears and her tail as the locusts clung to her fur and began to gnaw.

"Please!" she cried. "Stop it!"

There was no responding voice, only the onslaught of insects.

Breathstealer put her head down and plunged into the cloud, not consciously choosing a direction, but simply running as fast as her muddy paws would let her. She stumbled over rocks and ricocheted off tree trunks, and the locusts swarmed along with her, clinging to her fur and throwing themselves in her way. She snarled and snapped at them, crunching any that came within her jaws' reach and spitting them aside as she ran, but there were so many, and no escape.

Then suddenly her paws splashed into cold water, and she stumbled and fell, gasping and then choking on a mouthful of freezing, foul-smelling, weed-choked water. She surfaced again and began trying to swim, half-aware that the locusts probably couldn't follow her under the water. As bad as the smell was, for a moment she was glad of it, because it blocked out the dizzying stink of the Great Devourer's presence.

But she soon realized that she had only swapped one set of problems for another.

Though she kicked and pawed at the swamp, or river, or whatever it was she had found, she barely seemed to move. The water was thick and muddy, and long green strings of vegetation tangled around her paws. She couldn't feel the bottom now, and she began to panic, and as she did she felt her limbs twitching, thrashing, out of her control. She kicked and writhed and threw back her head with a desperate cry.

"Help!" she gasped. "Anyone, he—"

Then the water closed over her muzzle, and she couldn't find the surface, and her heart was trying to crawl up through her throat, and things began to go dark. . . .

I should have accepted its gift, she thought, and then she couldn't think anything at all.

4

Despite shouldering his way as close to the front of the crowd as he could, it still seemed to take a long time for the animals ahead of Stride to filter in to see the Great Mother. He paced back and forth, napped in a patch of sunlight, tried to ignore his rumbling stomach. Finally, as the afternoon was wearing on and the sun was sinking low in the sky, he knew he was almost there. The rhinoceros in front of him stood and shifted, anticipating its turn. He'd tried to talk to the morose creature earlier but came to regret it. Rhinos were grumpy at the best of times, but this one was monosyllabic and morose. Its complaint seemed to have nothing to do with the broken horn, but rather was about its skin. Stride wasn't sure how it expected the Great Spirit to intervene in such a matter.

There was a flurry of activity in one of the trees, and a

baboon swung down onto the high rock and waved her arms for their attention.

"Apologies, everyone. I'm afraid Great Mother Starlight has seen her last petitioner today," she cried. "Go home, if you can, and come back tomorrow."

A chorus of grumbling rose from the waiting crowd, and even a few hisses and snarls, though they were quickly shushed. The rhino snorted, thumped the ground with one enormous foot, and stomped off into the undergrowth, muttering something about an itch that would drive the Spirit itself mad.

Stride just stood and watched as the remaining creatures wandered away or settled down where they were to wait out the night. His pelt prickled with irritation, then with desperation.

No. I can't just wait another day. Starlight will understand. I just need to get to her.

He put on his best impression of a disappointed petitioner slinking away to lie down somewhere in the forest, turning away from the baboon and wandering into the trees, his tail drooping. Then as soon as he was out of sight, he paused, tasting the air. The scent of elephant was strong here, and there were several churned-up trails all over the forest, but he found Starlight's scent easily enough. After that, it wasn't hard to track her through the trees, ducking below the undergrowth whenever he heard baboons passing above just in case. It was oddly like stalking prey, stopping to listen for sounds that he'd been seen, trying to sense which way the wind was moving through the trees.

He heard her before he saw her, and he assumed she was still talking to the last animal she'd deigned to see that day—but at first, when he peered through the ferns, he couldn't see who she was speaking to. Was she talking to a vulture or another creature who didn't speak grasstongue? Or was she just having a conversation with herself? It wouldn't be the strangest thing a Great Parent had ever done. . . .

But then he caught movement, up by Starlight's enormous ear. Something was dangling from a branch right beside her head. It was a small bat, with dark gray wings and thick orange fur around its little fox-like head.

"From the graveyard? What kind of news?" Starlight said.

The bat's voice was almost too quiet and squeaky for Stride to hear, and he slunk closer, pressing his chest to the ground so he could crawl underneath a bush. He pricked and angled his ears to hear them better.

"They have never seen anything like it, Great Mother," the bat said. "An old elephant died a few days ago—Ravine was his name. He came to the graveyard with his family, as usual, and he lay down and died, and then . . ."

The bat twitched nervously, rubbing its wing-claws together.

"You can tell me," said Starlight.

"He didn't go to the stars. He went . . . somewhere else."

Stride's pelt rippled.

Starlight frowned, the folds of skin over her trunk deep enough to lose a mouse in. "I see. And was he a Codebreaker?"

"No, not that any of his family knew. We didn't tell them

what we saw exactly, it seemed . . . cruel. But we asked, as subtly as we could. It's not just Ravine, Great Mother. One of the flying foxes told me it's happened before."

"What has?"

The bat shuddered. "Animals all over Bravelands are dying and not going to the stars, when by all rights they should."

Starlight nodded very slowly.

She's not surprised, Stride thought a little angrily. *She knows something is going on, and she hasn't told anyone.*

"I have sensed something was wrong," Starlight told the little bat. "I did not know what it could be. . . . And when the spirits don't go to the stars, what does that look like?"

"Not good," squeaked the bat. "Like they're trying to go, but something has a grip on them and they can't escape. Like they're being . . . trapped."

Stride swallowed. It was as if his vision was being described exactly. *But does that mean . . . Flicker . . . ?*

"I'm only reporting what I saw," continued the bat. "And what others have told me."

"The eyes of your kind are special," said Starlight. "You see the threshold of life and death in a way no others can."

"What's happening?" asked the bat.

"I think I know who is responsible," Starlight said darkly. She paused for a moment, staring at something only she could see. "Thank you, dear friend. Go back to the flock and spread the word to be on the watch for these incidents. If you see any pattern to it, come and let me know. I will see what I can find out."

"All right," said the bat. "Dusk bring you joy, Great Mother."

And with that it took off, vanishing at once into the shadowy canopy of the trees.

Stride lay under his bush for a moment longer, trying to decide what to do. Part of him wanted to march out and confront the Great Mother, but could he persuade her to talk to him, even now? She might just keep things to herself, and how would that help Flicker?

"It's very rude to listen in on others' conversations," Starlight said, suddenly and sternly. "Come out here please, Stride."

Stride flinched and slunk out from beneath his bush, feeling like a cub who'd been disobeying his mother. He shook himself as he stood before her and let Flicker's face come back to his mind and fill him with anger, and with fear.

"You need to tell me what's going on," he said.

"Do I?" Starlight asked flatly. "When you disobey my wishes and sneak into my private conversations?"

"Yes," said Stride, flicking his tail in annoyance. "Because whatever's happening, it is happening to Flicker! I saw her last night in a dream, her spirit was—she was saying goodbye, but before she could go to the stars, something caught hold of her. It dragged her down into the earth! She was terrified! So yes, I think you do owe me an explanation, actually!"

Starlight's cold stare softened, and her ears flapped sadly as she let out a long breath. "Oh, Stride. I am terribly sorry. Of course . . . yes, I should have seen it, of course it would be connected. . . . Let me gather my thoughts for a moment, please, and then I will tell you what I know. I'm afraid it is not terribly much."

She went quiet again, dipping her enormous head and touching the grass with her trunk. Stride eventually relaxed, sitting back on his haunches, waiting for the Great Mother to gather her thoughts.

"What do you know of the Great Devourer, Stride?" she said at last.

Stride shivered. "Not much. It's something to do with the hyenas, isn't it?"

"It is the spirit that rules over all death in Bravelands. Long ago—so tells the story I know—the Great Devourer ruled Bravelands alone, before the Great Spirit came to foster life and protect living things. Death as we know it today is a natural force, random, arbitrary. The Great Devourer, though, became greedy. It *wanted* death. It actively sought ways to collect the spirits of living animals. There was no Code. Animals killed at a whim, and at the Devourer's whim."

Stride thought of the shadow, the one that chased every cheetah that ran too fast, the one that had caught Flicker, and he felt cold.

"When the Great Spirit came, it formed a balance—life and death in something more like harmony. The Great Parents established the Code. Only kill to survive. And the spirits of animals were no longer hoarded by the Devourer after death—instead, they went to the stars, to look down on Bravelands and remember.

"There have been many, many Codebreakers over the years, of course. Some, those whose presence in the stars would pain the Great Spirit, still belong to the Devourer, and the Devourer is still, will always be, the spirit of death in our lives. That is how I understand things."

"So . . . it's getting greedy again now?" Stride asked. "It's stealing spirits that should have gone to the stars?"

"I think that is very likely," said Starlight. She looked tired and suddenly very old. "I do not know why it would turn now against the way things have been for so long. Perhaps there was . . . hmm . . ."

"What?" Stride asked, hanging on her words.

"Once—a long time ago—a Great Mother was murdered. An elephant. She was killed in a plot that turned Bravelands upside down for a while. Stinger, the scheming baboon . . . Titan the heart-eater . . . the great snake, Grandmother . . ." Starlight shook her head. "We have always had Codebreakers, large and small. I do not know this for certain, but I wonder if the unnecessary deaths of so many have led to greater and greater evils—and now to this. The Devourer is awash with powerful spirits, and it wants more."

"Well, it can't have Flicker!" Stride said, leaping to his paws. "How do we get her back?"

Great Mother Starlight fixed him with a sad but steady look. "I don't know," she said. "I am not sure we can."

"So are you just going to stand here and do nothing?" Stride yowled, pacing in front of her, his tail twitching.

"No! I am going to do everything I can. But the Great Devourer is not a creature. He is not keeping Flicker and the others in a cave or a tree. We cannot face him directly. Only fight his malign influence where we find it."

"Then please," Stride begged, "tell me how to find him so I can fight him!"

Starlight's expression lightened, and Stride was irritated for a moment before she spoke. "I do have some good news for you, then. I think I know why you were brought to me. I need you to find out what has happened to a young buffalo calf."

"A buffalo?" Stride asked, thrown for a moment. "Is it dead too?"

"That is the question," said Starlight. "His name was Echo. He was chosen to lead his herd—a task that is vital, for the buffalo believe that if they do not migrate according to their secret ways, the rains will never come. A true drought would spell disaster for Bravelands—and many, many more deaths."

"I see," Stride breathed. Though he still couldn't really understand what this had to do with him, Flicker, or indeed the mysterious Great Devourer.

"Echo went missing. His herd believes him dead, but the vultures tell me they cannot find him. It could be that he *is* dead and has been taken by the Devourer, to somewhere the birds cannot find him. It could be that he is alive and lost. Find out, and perhaps we can set things right with the buffalo."

"And how will that bring Flicker back?" asked Stride.

"It won't," replied the Great Mother baldly. "Flicker is dead. You must accept that."

"But her spirit lives on," snapped Stride, "trapped in the Great Devourer's lair somewhere. I don't see how finding a buffalo calf will get her out."

Starlight shook her ears a little frustratedly. "Stride, the Great Spirit is telling me the two are connected. I don't know how, but somehow all this is linked."

Stride raked the ground with his claws. He couldn't put Flicker's face out of his mind. Would this really help her?

Starlight leaned over him and rested her trunk gently on the top of his head. He felt the weight of it, and it calmed him just a little. "Find patience," she said. "Just a little patience, and goodness will follow."

He looked up into her kind dark eyes that carried the weight of Braveland's troubles, yet seemed in that moment to see only his. There was no malice there, no deception. Only compassion. She had taken him in when he was in despair. He could at least do this for her. And if there was even a chance if would help Flicker too, it would be worth it.

"I'll do it," he said.

5

Whisper heard a rustling sound behind her and startled, kicking over rocks in her hurry to turn around.

Crossing the savannah with only Thunder and Bellow for company had been worrying enough—alone, it was terrifying. Every creaking tree and squeaking animal made her senses flare. She had passed the glinting river already—once she might have had to swim across, risking the biting jaws of crocodiles, but now it was so low that she could steel herself and make a run for it, and she was through the danger before any crocodiles that might have lain in the mud had sensed her.

She pressed on, trying not to think about the shield of larger buffalo she no longer had, trying not to imagine that there were lions and hyenas crouching in every patch of grass. The fact that she was actually *looking for* lions only made it worse. Her nerves were in knots when she heard the sound, and turned to find . . .

No lions. Just a small flock of birds approaching her. She relaxed, and then she caught her breath once more. These weren't just any birds. It was a group of oxpeckers. They flitted toward her, bobbing through the sky in an irregular hustle of wings, sometimes flying high, sometimes low. As they drew level with her, one flew down, landed on her short horns, and tapped with its tiny clawed foot.

"Have you come to help me?" she breathed, despite knowing that she couldn't understand the answer, and it probably couldn't understand the question either. "Wait, does . . . does that mean . . ."

The oxpecker took off again, up and away into the sky with the others. She watched them go, too stunned to move, until one circled back to her, around her head, and then flapped off to rejoin the others.

"Oh!" Whisper cried, and set off after them at a trot. Her heart in her mouth, her hopeless hope rising with the flight of the oxpeckers, she followed them across the dusty plain as they dipped and swam through the air. They seemed as if they had a direction they were leading her in, but they were also searching for something. . . .

It can't be.

It must be!

How could it be?

They led her around the edge of a large rock pile, and then suddenly she stopped, the scent of lions abruptly filling her nostrils. She instinctively backed off, her prey senses shouting at her to run from the danger—but a few tentative sniffs later, she realized the scent was a little faded, and she forced herself to look again.

There were no lions here, but clearly there had been, some time before. They had marked the rocks with their scent. The oxpeckers flitted down to land on the rocks and on the ground, prodding at it with their bright orange beaks. She saw tawny lion fur, scuffs on the dry earth, and—Whisper's breath caught painfully—a pile of bones, mostly picked clean.

But they weren't buffalo bones. Her breathing came back in a rush of relief. Even a tiny newborn calf wouldn't have a rib cage that size.

"Was Bellow right?" she muttered. "Was it a deer or something the lions were chasing, and not a buffalo at all? But then why are you here?" she said, frowning at the oxpeckers. One of them was hopping on the ground, whistling in what seemed like excitement. She peered down and realized that it was going in little circles around an imprint on the earth. A pawprint?

A *hoofprint*. Bigger than a deer's, the same size and shape as her own.

"There was a buffalo calf here!" she cried.

She checked the ground again, anxiously, looking for signs of spilled blood—the lions could have killed their prey here and dragged the carcass elsewhere to eat it. But she didn't see anything other than a faint staining of the earth beneath the bone pile.

Then, her heart in her mouth, she tried to follow the

hoofprints—but they vanished as she came out of the hollow and into thicker grass beyond.

"Where next?" she asked the oxpeckers. "Look above, see if you can see them!"

The oxpeckers were chattering to one another, and she sensed urgency from their whistling voices—but they didn't move.

"Well? Go on!" Whisper urged them again, but still the little birds didn't take off. Whisper stomped the ground in frustration. "Why did you bring me here, then, if you won't find him now?" she demanded.

The oxpeckers ruffled their feathers. One of them flapped down and perched on the white arch of a rib bone, fixing her with a brief beady stare, before starting to peck at the insects that crawled around the remains.

Whisper sagged. "I suppose I don't stand much of a chance against a pack of lions by myself. I need help. But now I know for sure there was a calf here . . . and *you* brought me here. . . . Maybe I can get help."

She perked up again as she came to a decision. She would go back and tell Thunder and Bellow what she'd found. Whatever else was happening here, there *was* a buffalo calf that had been in the same place as the lions, and it looked not to have been killed. She didn't understand why, but it meant there had to be hope he could still be rescued.

It might not be a male calf. It might not be him.

"Thank you," she told the oxpeckers.

Busy with their bone-picking, they did not respond.

* * *

She was about halfway back to where she had left the others, readying herself to cross the shallow river, when she felt the rumble under her hooves and stopped dead. She knew that sound-feeling. She cast around and spotted it on the horizon: a cloud of dust and a shadow that was hundreds of shadows moving.

The herd!

Her heart swelled without her permission, despite the painful knowledge that it wasn't *her* herd, not anymore—at least not at the moment. And then confusion crept in as she looked at the position of the cloud, considered how far they were now from the porcupine hill and the great ravine. Not far enough.

Surely even with the delay caused by Echo's disappearance and Bellow and Holler's duel, the herd should have gotten farther by now? She didn't know the secrets of the migration any more than Holler did—that knowledge was held by one and one alone—but she was fairly sure this was not where the herd was supposed to be.

She had to know what was going on.

It wasn't too hard to approach the herd—even as she began to draw close, the other buffalo barely seemed to notice her. A single young female, catching up with a giant migrating herd, wasn't going to make much of a stir, at least at first. But Whisper was still nervous as she came close enough to hear the conversation of some of the buffalo. She had left the herd, and not quietly, spurning Holler in front of many witnesses.

Would they drive her away if they recognized her?

For now, she approached carefully from behind, and they didn't seem to see her at all. One of the larger females was complaining loudly to the others in a strident voice.

"Locusts!" she was hooting. "We never ran into locusts last year! Locusts and drought, and now *this*." She hoofed the ground in disgust, and Whisper looked down to see that the grass underfoot was so dry, it was crumbling at the lightest touch. The buffalo tried to take a bite, but it practically turned to dust before she could swallow it.

"I don't understand," said a smaller male, a youth about Quake's age. "We just came past here, and it was fine! Why did we turn back this way if there was nothing to eat?"

"I understand perfectly," muttered another female.

"Shhhh, Tremble," said an older female. "You know he's got ears everywhere."

"So? Let him hear!" snapped Tremble. "He's doing a bad job!"

"Tremble, no," said the louder female, suddenly shouldering Tremble aside. "You know what happened to Rattle!" She looked up, now facing Whisper, and frowned. "Oh, it's you!" she said. "Come to your senses yet? Here to ask Holler to take you back?"

"No," said Whisper. "I have news that affects the herd . . . but what was that you were saying about the migration?"

All the buffalo shuffled their hooves and looked awkward.

"Nothing. It's going fine," said the young male. He was half again as tall as Whisper, but he still withered under the glare she gave him. "We've had a few problems, but we're on the right trail now," he muttered.

"So I was right," Whisper said. "Holler's not our rightful leader, and his guidance is steering you all toward disaster." She took a deep breath, steeling herself. *I might be wrong—but this is wrong, too. So let me be wrong.* "What would you say if I told you Echo was still alive? If he was lost somewhere nearby?"

Tremble's eyes widened, but the others just shook their heads or stamped nervously and looked away.

"Better not let Holler see you here, saying things like that," said the older female. "Go on, shoo, or you might regret it."

"Too late," said a voice. Whisper looked up and saw a familiar bulky young male stomping toward them. *Quake . . .*

She drew herself up, raising her head defiantly, and stared him down as he approached. The very sight of him made her twitch with rage on the inside. She felt as if she was back in that quicksand in the dark, forcing herself to stand still, listening to Murmur cry out with fear and panic as her desperate writhing dragged her down to her death.

"What do you want here, Whisper?" Quake asked, hitching his horns. "My father won't like it if you're just here spreading more silly rumors."

"I don't care what your father likes or what you say," Whisper said, shaking off the awful memories. "It's clear this migration is going just as badly as I thought it would, and I bring news that the herd deserves to hear."

"Then come with me and deliver it straight to him, if you dare," Quake sneered. He turned his back, gesturing her to follow with another toss of his horns. To think she'd once actually found him almost attractive, under the bluster and arrogance. But that was all he was—arrogance born of being the herd leader's son. She sniffed and fell in line behind him, and they made their way deeper into the herd, until they were passing through a thick crowd of buffalo who all turned to stare at her. She suddenly felt nervous, as if she was surrounded by enemies and being led to their leader for interrogation or punishment. She bristled against the feeling, raising her voice so they could all hear.

"Do you think it was worth it, Quake?" she asked.

"Was what worth it?" he grumbled back.

"Murdering Murmur," Whisper snarled, to gratifying gasps from the watching herd. "Was it worth killing her for this? What about setting the hyenas on Echo and wounding Bellow so he won't last out the season? Was this failed migration worth the deaths of three good and kind buffalo?"

Quake rounded on her. "Lies!" he snapped. "Murmur's death was a mistake."

Whisper simply stood and stared him down once more in silence.

I said what I said, she thought. *I want the others to know, but I don't need to convince you, do I, Quake? You know what you did.*

Quake glared back at her, his sides almost shaking. He seemed, surprisingly, upset.

Then he spat on the ground and turned his back on her again. Whisper felt a dark thrill of satisfaction as he walked away. Forcing Quake to face his crime wouldn't help Murmur, or Echo, or Bellow. But it certainly made her feel better.

It was immediately clear when they were approaching Holler's inner circle of buffalo. Firstly, the number of females dwindled to just a few of the biggest and strongest. Secondly, they entered a patch of grass that was much better quality, maybe watered by some underground source that hadn't yet dried up. Most of the herd were gathered around it, but outside it, including the elderly and most of the calves, but Holler and his cronies were grazing happily, ignoring the rest.

Of course, Whisper thought. *He thinks that being a leader allows special privileges.*

"Father," Quake said. "Whisper has returned. She claims to have . . . news."

Holler's head shot up, and he snorted angrily. "Whisper?"

He stomped slowly over to her, the ground shaking as his massive form drew closer. Whisper tried to give him the same raised chin and unswerving gaze as she had his son, but it was a lot harder. His huge horns could have tossed her into the air as if she was made of twigs.

"How is my brother faring?" he asked, his voice cold.

Whisper didn't want to give him the satisfaction of the truth—that Bellow was in dire straits, humiliated, weak, and in all likelihood dying. "He worries for the herd, as always."

"Well, he needn't," said Holler. "They are in good spirits and good health."

Whisper glanced about at the better fed among the group. "Well, some of them are," she muttered.

A rumble came from Holler's throat. "Enough pleasantries.

Are you spying on us, little calf? Go back to Bellow and tell him we won't fall for his tricks that easily."

Whisper wrinkled her nose. "I'm not here for Bellow. I'm here for myself." She took a deep breath. She was about to commit to her story, and if it turned out she was wrong—well, so be it. "I'm here for Echo. He's alive."

Holler chuckled nastily, and he seemed to relax, as if he'd realized he didn't have to take her seriously at all. "This again? You poor, deluded calf. It must be so hard, losing your little brother in such a tragic accident. Some buffalo escort this lost child back to her own herd."

He began to turn away.

"The Great Spirit's judgment will find the herd," Whisper called out. She couldn't lose him now—more important, she couldn't lose the buffalo who were listening. "If we abandon Echo now, after everything, when the migration is failing, we will deserve everything that comes to us. You are already lost! You all know you're not supposed to be here! The rains are no closer than they ever were, and if you don't do something soon, you'll starve."

There was an awkward shuffling. Whisper took a big breath and hurried on before anyone could stop her.

"The oxpeckers never chose a new leader. They spent all their time roosting in the tree by the ravine where he fell, instead of coming on the migration with all of you. Don't you wonder why? Well, I know. I heard from creatures on the plains that a lone buffalo calf was traveling with a lion pride—not being hunted by them, just traveling with them. And then the oxpeckers led me to an empty lion den, and it's true, there was a calf there. Why would the oxpeckers care if it wasn't our lost leader? Why would a lion pride not kill a buffalo calf on sight?"

Holler was shaking his head. "This is nonsense. And we are not lost."

"I don't know for sure," Whisper said, turning to appeal to the other buffalo. "But isn't it worth finding out? If your true, chosen leader could be out there, after all you've been through recently, wouldn't it be wise to look? What kind of leader would abandon all hope without trying?"

"A wise one," snorted one of Holler's cronies. "A sensible one who doesn't run off after calves' tales!"

Holler looked like he was about to speak again, but he stopped, his tail twitching and his nostrils flaring.

"Lions!" hissed one of the other buffalo.

Whisper spun around, sniffing the air. She could smell it too—the scent of predators.

"Form the Shield!" Holler shouted. "Circle the calves!"

Despite his corruption, despite the rumblings of discontent among the herd, the buffalo snapped into action at Holler's call, and the next thing Whisper knew she was in the circle of a storm of huge, hairy bodies. The calves and elderly buffalo of the herd were quickly encircled by several rings of bigger, stronger animals. Whisper would normally be swept up with the calves, but this time she ignored the call of safety—instead she stuck close to Holler, knowing he would be at the forefront, facing off against the lions. Her heart pounded with fear but thrilled with a kind of excitement at the same time.

It can't be a coincidence . . . can it?

Sure enough, standing on the outer ring near Holler, almost squashed between the shoulders of the biggest and the strongest buffalo in the herd, Whisper saw the lithe, tawny shape of a lioness crossing the plain toward them.

"*She* led them here," muttered one of the older buffalo with a scornful glance at Whisper.

"So?" snapped Tremble from over her shoulder. "It's only one lion. She won't dare threaten the herd." Whisper realized the adult female had followed her here, and she was grateful to have someone on her side.

She was right, there was no way a single lion would even approach the great herd under normal circumstances—and yet this lion was pacing straight for them. She was not running, not stalking, but keeping her head up and her ears forward, as if they were old friends.

"Greetings," she said, stopping a few buffalo-lengths away from the outer circle, addressing the solid wall of hoof and horn with a slight bow. "I wish to speak to the leader of this herd."

The buffalo around Holler took small steps back, exposing him.

"Enough of this nonsense," snarled Holler. "You wish to say something to me, cat?" He stomped forward, and a few of the largest males followed him, peeling from the circle and forming up around the lion. Whisper scrambled after them, though it took a great effort to override her instincts and run *with* the big aggressive buffalo, *toward* the predator. "Leave, now," Holler snorted, thumping the ground with his hoof. "Or we'll turn your bones to dust."

"Holler, I presume," said the lion. She didn't look scared, though surely she must have been. "My name is Fearsome, of Noblepride, and I think you want to hear what I have to say. My pride has found something I think your herd mislaid."

Whisper could hardly breathe.

"Mislaid?" said Holler.

The lion chuckled. "Indeed. A princeling buffalo."

Whisper's heart was thumping almost too loud in her ears for her to hear the lion's next words, but she saw in the eyes of the other buffalo that they had all heard it.

"He says his name is Echo."

6

Burning air and blinding light burst into Breathstealer's dark world. She didn't even feel the teeth in her fur at first, as she gasped in a long and painful breath. Then, like a cub, she felt herself being lifted, dragged through the water by the fur at the nape of her neck. She thrashed instinctively, pounding the water with her paws until she felt soft mud beneath them, then pulling herself up and out, collapsing breathless on the banks of the swamp.

She still heard insects buzzing, and for a moment she tensed—but it was only the chatter of swamp creatures. The brain-melting buzzing of the locusts had gone.

She did hear something else, though. Breathing—no, *panting*—right behind her.

She sat up at once, staggering to all fours, pawing at her face to try to clear the muck from her eyes. In front of her, there

EAST MOLINE PUBLIC LIBRARY

was a kind of creature she had glimpsed before, but never so close up.

It was a wolf. A sleek shape, as big as she was, with pointed ears and a pelt of mottled gold and gray. She startled as she looked into its eyes and saw they were milky white, as if she was looking into a thick bank of cloud.

"Are you all right?" said the wolf. "You're a hyena, aren't you?" He sniffed at her. "Yes, even through the bog-water, I know that smell. What in the Spirit's sight happened to you?"

"I . . . I fell into the water," Breathstealer gasped. How could she tell this stranger the real truth? She'd been running from a cloud of locusts who spoke with the voice of Death. . . . "I caught my paw on some reeds." She coughed up a mouthful of swamp water and sputum. "Thank you for helping me!"

"I heard you thrashing about and yelling," said the wolf, sitting down and scratching his side with his back paw. "To be honest, I thought you might be something edible." He gave her a wide, wolfy grin.

"Lucky for me," Breathstealer said, trying to sound confident and eyeing the bank of the bog around her, wondering if he was really blind, and which would be the best way to run. . . . "Not even lions like the taste of hyena."

The wolf chuckled. "Only hyenas eat hyena, from what I've heard," he said.

"Not by preference," said Breathstealer.

The wolf didn't seem to be about to attack her. And surely it would have done by now, if it meant to eat her. She fancied her chances in a fight, though—it could only have weighed as

EAST MOLINE PUBLIC LIBRARY

much as a small hyena male.

"My name's Breathstealer," she said.

"They call me Graypelt," said the wolf.

"And are you . . . can you . . . see me?" Breathstealer asked, stumbling over the urge to be polite to the creature that had saved her.

"No," said Graypelt, cheerfully. "Blind as a rock. But twice as hard to kill," he added with another wide grin. "My pack would have kept me fed and safe, but I prefer to live alone. I like this place. It would not suit a pack, but the prey here is both bountiful and extremely noisy."

"Then we have something in common," said Breathstealer, relaxing a little. "I'm packless too." Though she wasn't sure he was telling the complete truth about the prey in this place—he looked malnourished to her. "Well, I'm ravenous," she said. "I'm going to find some food. You're welcome to join me, it's the least I can do."

Graypelt dipped his head in acknowledgment.

The bushpig gave a last twitch and went still in Breathstealer's jaws. She gave it one more shake and then dragged it across the boggy stream to the wolf's territory. She was drooling by the time she heard the sniffing and Graypelt pushed through the ferns toward her. This place no longer stank of death, as it had just before the Great Devourer had come to her, but it didn't smell great—the delicious scent of the bushpig's blood was a welcome change.

Graypelt fell upon the prey, feeding as if he had not had a

good meal in many moons. Breathstealer ate her share, but she made sure that there was plenty left for the wolf.

"So," he said. "How did a strong young hyena end up pack-less?"

"I . . . didn't fit in with the others," said Breathstealer. "I tried, but in the end I decided to leave. I didn't really mean to come here, I was following . . . some prey. And then I got lost."

It's not so far from the truth, really, she told herself. *I tried to be a good clan-mate. But I decided to stand up to my mother and the others, so I was exiled.*

And as for what happened to her in the jungle . . . a cold shiver ran through her when she recalled the Great Devourer's words, its offer, the feeling of *wrongness*.

"Well, I would welcome such a good hunter to live in my jungle, if you were willing to share your prey." Graypelt chuckled. "But I assume you would prefer to be shown the way out of this forest."

"I would," Breathstealer said. Though where she would go next, she didn't know. She had clearly enraged the Great Devourer and wondered what that might mean for her future.

"Then eat up and follow me," said Graypelt. "And we will go together."

They finished their meal in short order and set out. The journey out of the jungle was longer, but much calmer than the journey in. Graypelt's nose and his careful paws led them surely and steadily through the bog and between the ferns. She marveled at his agility in spite of his blindness. He slipped through the dappled shadows, as insubstantial as mist, and once or twice seemed to vanish completely, becoming one with the foliage. The air grew warmer and drier as they climbed a gentle slope that seemed to go on for much longer than the one Breathstealer had come down in the other direction. Glimmering golden light began to stab down through openings in the canopy, as they passed by hives of buzzing insects, nests of little creatures that got out of Graypelt's way with a chorus of squeaking and scampering.

The ground grew dry, and the leaves crunched beneath their paws. As they finally emerged, Breathstealer blinked in the glare of the late-day sun and almost wished she could go back to the deep jungle, where at least it was cool, and there was plenty to drink if you didn't mind it being thick with mud and weeds and insects.

But she couldn't go back. She knew it was irrational—the Great Devourer was everywhere, could see her anywhere, had sent its insects to her plenty of times out in the open air. But she still gave a small sigh of relief to feel the moving air on her fur.

She looked over at Graypelt, who was sniffing the air with interest, apparently enjoying the play of the wind on his face too. Once again she frowned at how thin he was, even more pronounced now that his belly was full of bushpig.

It's none of my business if he wants to stay in the jungle and eat nothing but tiny lizards, she told herself. *What kind of help can I offer him anyway, clanless and alone and with . . . with everything that just happened to me?*

But she couldn't just walk off and leave him. She didn't want to.

"Do you really like the jungle?" she said.

"I do," said Graypelt, but his tone suggested there were limits to his love of it.

"It's been so nice for me," she went on, "having someone to talk to. And I can't forget what you did for me. If you'd be willing to come with me—two packless creatures together—I would like that."

She was trying to save his pride, of course, but she found that she wasn't lying either. Graypelt was good company. And perhaps more to the point, having a purpose, a goal, to keep a friend alive . . . maybe it would give her more of a reason to keep going. To hold on to her life, in defiance of . . . whatever it was the Great Devourer wanted from her.

And he seems wise, she thought. *Maybe I can tell him the truth. . . .*

"All right," said Graypelt happily, with very little hesitation at all. He sniffed the air. "Where shall we go? Lead on, my friend!"

They skirted the forest for a while. Breathstealer had noticed creatures crowding into the shade, taking less care to be stealthy in their desire to get out of the burning sun, and they caught a few small pieces of prey as they traveled. Breathstealer carried a few spiny mice in her jaws as they peeled away from the trees and headed out over the plains, and when they lay down for the night under a small rocky overhang, she stashed them in a corner for the morning.

Graypelt talked as he was falling asleep. He told her about his life with his pack before he decided to leave, and he was halfway through a story about following a scent that turned out to be going in circles, when he went quiet and began to snore.

Breathstealer stared into the starry sky, turning her encounter with the Devourer over and over in her mind.

Perhaps you do not truly understand the power we are offering. . . .

Well, that was certainly right. She did not understand. The power over life and death? Why should she be promised such a thing? And why had it felt so important not to accept?

Why did the Great Devourer sound so angry about the Great Spirit?

She did not think they were *friends*. She didn't consider that they might have *feelings* about each other in that way at all. She never thought they might be enemies. What would that even mean? How could you be *against* death?

The other hyenas in the clan had always distrusted her visions—thinking she was delirious, or worse, simply making things up. And for a long time, she'd simply been confused by the things she'd half seen in the insect swarms. Really, the so-called gift had never brought her anything but grief. It was a power of sorts, but one she didn't know how to yield. If it was the future she was witnessing in her visions, it was only a version of it, muddled and hazy as the horizon on a sunbaked day.

She shuddered, imagining that she heard the buzzing of the locust cloud again.

Except she wasn't imagining.

Something really was buzzing. A flicker of insect wings caught the edge of her vision, and she startled, casting about in the darkness to see where it had come from. For a moment she saw nothing and heard nothing. Then, right in front of her face, the largest moth she had ever seen soared out of the dark. It beat its wings around her eyes and her muzzle, surprisingly strong for a creature so delicate, and Breathstealer cringed back, squeezing her eyes shut.

The beating of the wings went on a moment longer, and then they stopped. Breathstealer looked up and shuddered.

She was no longer in the darkness under the rocky overhang. She was standing in front of the great baobab, the tree where the hyena clan lived. She was looking at the dens between the roots, where her mother and the other favored hyenas slept, surrounded by other hyenas lying out under the stars. It was no longer the dark of night, but it wasn't day either—a strange, even blue twilight seemed to cover the land in front of her. Everything was completely, unnaturally still. She couldn't see the sleeping hyenas breathing, but she didn't think they were dead—it was as if time had stopped for a moment. The baobab's branches were eerily frozen too, and there was no sound at all.

Until red light flared from one of the sleeping dens. It flickered and danced, one minute not there, the next a wild and roaring flame. And with the flame came the sound of a hyena screaming in pain.

Mother! Breathstealer gasped, trying to run toward the fire, but her paws made no contact with the frozen earth, and she gained no ground. She knew it was her mother in that den, her mother's voice crying out in agony, but she couldn't get to her—

She snapped back to herself, and for a moment the darkness around her seemed absolute—though in a moment her eyes readjusted, and she saw the stars overhead and heard her own ragged breathing. The moth was gone.

"What's wrong?" said Graypelt's voice from the overhang behind her.

For a moment, Breathstealer couldn't think how to answer that.

"I had a dream," she began. "I dreamed about my mother.... There was a fire in her den, back where the clan sleeps. She was in agony...."

Graypelt yawned and put out a paw, which gently tapped on her tail. "I am sorry. But it's best not to put too much faith in dreams," he said. "I'm sure your mother is fine."

Breathstealer sighed heavily, settled down, and tucked her legs beneath her body, shuddering.

"It's not just a dream," she said. She steadied herself. She had to tell someone the whole truth. Why not this strange, blind new friend? "I have these . . . visions. They come to me in swarms of insects, and I see things that are true, or might be true in the future, or are . . . versions of things that might happen. They're real. And they're sent by the Great Devourer," she said, dropping her voice to a hollow whisper.

She expected disbelief from Graypelt, but he didn't challenge her—he didn't even speak, just edged a little closer so she could feel the warmth of his fur near hers.

"The Devourer led me to your jungle. It led me to a swarm of locusts, and it *spoke* to me. I thought it might explain the visions, but it just said . . . it said . . ." She tried to clearly recall the words. "It seemed to be saying that they were a gift for me to use or not, as I wished. But they are real."

Why would it still send me these "gifts" now that I've refused its offer? Was I wrong to refuse after all?

Will I ever be rid of them?

But those were questions that could wait.

"I saw my mother's death, and I've seen death before— when the old clan leader died at my mother's jaws. I can't ignore this. I have to go back to the clan and warn them."

"Do you think they will believe you?" asked Graypelt quietly. He didn't sound at all as if he didn't believe her. He sounded genuinely concerned.

"I don't know," she said. "They might just drive me off. I didn't leave by myself at all; I was exiled."

"I suppose we will find out," said Graypelt.

"You—you don't have to come," Breathstealer said. She knew he could keep up, but against a determined clan of distrustful and hungry hyenas, a lone wolf wouldn't stand much of a chance even if he could see perfectly. And yet she felt a deep relief when he shook his head.

"I know. But I will," he said decisively. "I prefer to be of some help when I can. Wake me at dawn, and we will go."

Breathstealer settled down, letting the tension out of her lungs with a long breath. In the morning, she would face her clan again, but with Graypelt by her side, it didn't feel like such a terrifying task.

As she was drifting into sleep, it occurred to her to think that it wasn't exactly a usual thing for a wolf—any wolf, let alone one who'd chosen the life of a lone wolf—to *prefer to be of some help.*

Then sleep overtook her, and fitful dreams stole the thought away.

7

"Oi, where you off to?"

Stride's steps faltered as he heard Stonehide's voice behind him.

He had left the Great Mother's forest at dawn, and he hadn't stopped to tell the honey badger where he was going. They hadn't spoken since their last argument, and Stride hadn't felt like trying to explain everything Starlight had said to him. If he managed to find this buffalo calf—if he could even locate the wandering buffalo herd—and if he could find out the truth and come back to report to Starlight, then he had planned to find Stonehide again to talk.

But Stonehide clearly hadn't wanted to wait.

Even at a steady pace, he was faster than a honey badger— which suggested that Stonehide had been hustling to catch up. Stride slowed his steps, just a little.

"Hang on," panted Stonehide, coming alongside him. "Slow down, you great leggy menace!"

Stride sighed. "I don't need any company for this," he muttered. "The Great Mother has sent me on a mission, but I don't even know if it's possible."

"I know," said Stonehide. "If you'd wait for a minute before running off, you'd know Starlight told me to come with you."

"What?" Stride frowned, turning on Stonehide. "You?"

"Well, someone's got to keep an eye on you," Stonehide sniffed.

"I don't need an eye on me," he said. He was about to add, *and certainly not the eye of a Codebreaker*, but stopped himself. He didn't even know if the rumors were true.

But why did those creatures call him that if it's not?

Certainly, it was no surprise Stonehide hadn't mentioned it himself. It was hardly a badge of pride to have killed in cold blood, breaking the most fundamental law of the plains. Normally, Stride would have stayed well away, and it would have been easy too if Stonehide hadn't helped him so generously.

But something else troubled him, and it related to the stories Starlight had recounted. Codebreakers were dear to the Great Devourer, the source of Flicker's predicament. In the back of his mind, Stride couldn't shake the idea that Stonehide was somehow involved, even responsible for Flicker's spirit not ascending to the stars with her ancestors. Why Starlight would have thought the honey badger a suitable companion made little sense.

"I'm the one who's going to keep you on the right path,"

Stonehide said, as if reading his doubts. "Looking for a buffalo calf who might not exist? Too right you need help."

Stride gave his head a hard shake. "I *don't* need help, and I don't need watching like I'm a cub! You're not my mother, you're just some weird creature I met once. Tell Starlight I'll find Echo by myself."

"Oh, don't be like that," said Stonehide. "You're too cocky for your own good."

"And you're only going to slow me down," Stride retorted.

He didn't hang around to hear what Stonehide's reply would be. He leaped into a run, a measured speed at first, then faster and faster, until he could feel the wind passing over his fur, and he knew that he had left Stonehide far behind him. Let him try to keep up, if he cared so much about finding this buffalo. By the time he did, Stride would have found Echo and brought him to Starlight, and he would have found out how a missing calf and a dangerous long dry spell could even have anything to do with Flicker and the Great Devourer anyway. If it could be done, he would do it. That would show Starlight he was serious about helping Flicker.

The buffalo herd weren't too hard to track, once he had made his way to the ravine the Great Mother spoke of, and found the fading traces of them. If they'd set off on their migration on time, they might have gone too far to follow this way, but the ground was still rich with their scent and there were plenty of patches of churned-up mud, trampled plants, and grass that had been grazed almost to nothing.

The herd crossed other animals' territories with no heed

of danger—what could stop, let alone hurt, a huge number of animals that size? Crocodiles would take the weak and foolish, and lions might snatch the odd calf, but such was the death toll all grass-eaters paid to migrate. Stride didn't have that advantage of bulk and weight, but he did have speed. He went a little out of his way to avoid the strongest lion scents, but when he sensed the presence of other cheetahs he decided to cut straight across. What were the chances that they would run into each other?

He was unlucky. He rounded a small hill and was surprised to see two young cheetahs watching him from the branches of a yellow-leafed tree. They leaped down and padded straight for him, their tails twitching. Stride tried to size them up as they approached, wondering if they were allies or enemies. It was a pair of males, a little younger than him—probably recently joined a coalition, or maybe they were a coalition on their own.

They didn't look angry. They weren't running at him with the kind of protective fury of a coalition chasing off interlopers. But there was something in their eyes, in the pricking of their ears and tails, that he didn't quite like.

"Greetings, friends," he said when they got close enough to hear him. He put on a resolutely cheerful expression. "I'm following the buffalo herd. They went this way—a few days ago, was it?"

"You're on our territory," said one of the strange cheetahs with a moody curl of his lip.

So much for that.

It might only be posturing, thought Stride. Best keep the tone civil.

"I'm only passing through," Stride said. "Like I said, I'm following the buffalo. On an errand for the Great Mother," he added, though he had an awkward feeling that saying it aloud made it sound less impressive than it should. "Good day." He tried to walk around the two cheetahs and just keep going—they would see he wasn't planning to hunt here, and if they wanted to follow him all the way to the herd just to make sure, let them.

They stood and watched him, unblinking, until he had passed them. Then he heard the shifting of paws.

"Wait," said one of the young cheetahs.

Stride's heart sank.

"Why are you looking for the buffalo?" said the other.

"What does it have to do with the Great Mother?"

"Why would she pick you?"

"And how come you're alone?"

The two of them began to shadow his steps, peppering him with questions without waiting for answers, like annoying cubs. Stride tried to treat them as such and simply ignore them—but there was a sniggering malice in their voices that he did not like at all. They weren't about to let up.

He was starting to feel uncomfortable having these two at his back, when one of them finally said, "We know who you are."

"Stride," snarled the other. "The traitor."

So the news had traveled far and wide, across territory

boundaries. This changed matters, Stride realized with a trickle of dread. What could have been a brief unpleasant encounter might now easily turn to something far more serious.

"You betrayed your coalition," said the first one. "You stole your leader's mate."

Stride rounded on them. "Flicker was not Jinks's mate. She was *never* Jinks's mate."

"Think we care about the details? We're here for the bounty, not your life story."

Stride began to back away. The others followed, keeping pace. They weren't in the mood for a discussion, and he was fine with that. How could they ever begin to understand what had happened with Flicker? They were young. Foolish and full of blood. They'd never been in love.

"So Jinks has other cheetahs out here doing his dirty work for him?" he said. He was buying time. There were two of them—they were younger than him, but he wasn't sure if that would give him the advantage or them. Despite his pride, they might easily be as fast as he was. "If you kill me, you'll be Codebreakers, and Starlight will find you."

"Oh, we don't have to kill you," one said. "We'll get our reward if we just hobble you."

"So you can't run," said the other. "Or hide, or hunt. You just limp on until you starve, or the hyenas bring you down. Nothing to do with us."

A shudder ran down Stride's spine, rippling his pelt.

Did these two know about his brother? They probably

didn't. They wouldn't know that he had spent years caring for a cheetah who had been hobbled in an accident, watching him waste away despite Stride's efforts, robbed of his life's purpose.

But Jinks did know.

Stride growled at the two cheetahs as they slowly started to circle him. "Do you think it'll be that easy?" he snarled. But he knew that his fur was standing on end.

One of the cheetahs made a lazy swipe at his heels, barely even trying to hit him, but he was forced to skitter away from them, baring his teeth. Already, the other one was circling the other way to try to go for his back legs. Panic rising in his chest, Stride leaped for the first cheetah, claws out. He had to get them to back off. The young male seemed a little surprised at the move and was almost too late to duck out of the way—Stride's claws dragged across his muzzle, drawing a few drops of blood from a shallow scratch.

He spun at once, his ears twitching as he sensed the movement behind him. The second cheetah's lunge missed his back legs and caught him in the ribs instead. Stride dug his paws into the dirt and tried to stay upright, but the force of the blow sent both of them tumbling to the ground. He twisted his neck around and bit down hard on the cheetah's shoulder, the only part he could reach. The cheetah yelped and scrambled off him, shaking his head.

But the other one was back, and before Stride could get up he had thrown his whole weight down onto his side, lying across his neck. Stride sprawled back and then tried again to get up, snapping and clawing furiously but not quite getting a grip on the cheetah pinning him down. . . .

"Get him!" the cheetah yowled. "Get him, Scramble!"

"Hold him down," snarled Scramble, and Stride kicked and writhed with desperate strength, unable to even lift his head to see as the cheetah approached. . . .

Then there was a yelp of pain from Scramble and a sound of claws scratching on the earth.

"What is *that*?" said the cheetah on top of Stride. Stride managed to wriggle his paws underneath him and push up, shoving the cheetah off while he was distracted.

"It's got me!" Scramble yelled. "Get it off! Get it off!"

"It's only little," sneered the other cheetah, though he was backing away now, his ears pinned back. "Get it yourself."

"Only little, eh?" said a voice that was familiar, even through a mouthful of fur. "Take your tail back then, if you can."

Stonehide.

Stride managed to get up and turned to aim another swipe at the cheetah who had pinned him down. He caught it across the nose again, and it backed away some more, growling.

Scramble was turning in panicky circles now, trying to get a bite on the honey badger who had grabbed on to his tail. But Stonehide was as quick as him, and apparently stronger—when Scramble tried to pull his tail away, Stonehide dug in his claws and the cheetah went absolutely nowhere, no matter how hard he tugged.

"Let go!" Scramble yowled. "Or you'll regret it."

"Doubt it," said Stonehide. "How about you leave my

cheetah friend alone, and I don't scratch out your eyes?"

He finally let go, just as Scramble gave another huge tug on his tail, and the cheetah went sprawling in the dust. Stride came around to Stonehide's side.

"Get up, Scramble!" sneered the second cheetah, glaring at his friend as he licked his tail. "This isn't over," he added to Stride. "You can never stop running, ever again. Enjoy your life while you can, and don't go anywhere without your little mad friend, will you?"

And with that, he and Scramble turned tail and walked away. Stride could see them holding their heads up and not looking back, trying to preserve their dignity, despite being defeated by a creature less than half their size.

Stride waited silently by Stonehide's side until they had passed behind a tree and disappeared. Stonehide didn't look at him but gazed placidly after the retreating cheetahs.

Then Stride sniffed and scuffed the ground with one paw. "I, um . . . look, I . . . ," he muttered.

"Don't need you to thank me," Stonehide said coolly.

"Well. Thanks anyway," said Stride. "I was wrong."

"I know," said Stonehide. "So, where to now?"

8

She could not believe it.

Echo's alive.

All Holler's bluster and fury couldn't stop the news spreading through the herd, in mutters and in shouts, echoing the chaos inside Whisper's own mind.

Echo's alive.

She tried to focus. The lion was here, she was still talking. Echo might be alive, but now his fate lay in the claws of Noblepride. . . .

"I come to make you an offer," Fearsome said. She still seemed calm, and she spoke in a voice soft enough that the buffalo had to lean in to listen. Still, did Whisper detect a slight shiver in her limbs? After all, it would be the work of moments for the buffalo herd to turn on her, tossing her body from horns to hooves. *She knows she has something precious. . . .*

"Noble knows this princeling is important to you, so he offers you a deal," continued the lioness. "We will return Echo to your herd, and in return, you send us three of your buffalo. We secure the future of your herd, and you feed my pride for the rainy season."

A shocked quiet chased Echo's name from the mouths of the buffalo. Whisper felt a chill, despite the heat of the day.

They want us to send three buffalo to their deaths? We can't do that!

But we need Echo back. . . . Bravelands itself needs us to get him back. . . .

Holler's breath had been coming hard and angry through his nostrils ever since the lion had said Echo was alive. Now he let out a harsh laugh.

"Why would I make such a trade?" he demanded. "Echo is not so special I will sacrifice three buffalo for his sake. He is a calf. We lose hundreds of calves to your kind every year. What will one more hurt us?"

"But he's not an ordinary calf," Whisper put in, her voice coming out squeaky with nerves. She couldn't believe she was arguing for something so awful, but she simply *had* to stand up for Echo. *I couldn't save him before. There must be a way to do it now that I have this chance. . . .*

"Silence," Holler snapped. "You are no buffalo of this herd. If you don't hold your tongue I'll treat you like the interloper you are!"

Whisper shivered and looked around at the other buffalo, hoping they would back her up. Most of them believed Echo was the rightful leader. All of them should have some compassion for a lost calf in danger! But the others seemed to be avoiding her gaze.

"It would be wise to consider my offer," said Fearsome. She remained composed, but from the way she licked her lips, Whisper guessed this wasn't going quite the way she had hoped or expected. Whisper found herself wondering whether Fearsome had volunteered for this role, or whether she had been coerced. If Holler refused, she would go back empty-handed. If she managed to return at all. Several of the male buffalo by Holler's side were snorting and gouging the ground with their hooves, as if eager to teach this visitor a deadly lesson.

"And *you*," Holler rumbled, and as he turned back to the lion he stomped the ground with his own hooves, sending up clouds of dust and making the earth shake. He tossed his horns and raised his whole front half into the air, then thumped down closer to the lion, closer and closer, until Whisper thought she would be trampled. Fearsome held out longer than Whisper would have, but at last she flinched and scrambled away, her superior reflexes letting her escape Holler's reach for now. She ran, not directly away, but making a wide circle so that she could pause and call back.

"Take our deal, or the princeling dies," she growled.

"Wait," Whisper gasped. She pushed her way past Holler, risking being trampled herself, and ran after the lion. "Wait!"

Fearsome turned her predator eyes on Whisper, and Whisper shuddered, suddenly painfully aware that she had left the safety of the herd, that she was facing a creature who could and would kill her. . . .

EAST MOLINE PUBLIC LIBRARY

"Echo is my little brother," she called out. "Please, don't hurt him."

"*Please* won't fill my pride's bellies," said Fearsome.

"I'll figure something out," Whisper said. "I'll . . . I'll make sure you get something in return."

But what? she thought. *The lions want only one thing—flesh.*

Fearsome regarded her with bright yellow eyes. "You have until sunset," she said, and then she turned tail and scampered off, away from the herd, until she was lost in the dusty landscape.

Whisper hesitated a moment before she turned back to face the herd.

What can I do?

The herd could trample a pride of lions if Holler wished it—but wouldn't that be breaking the Code? And anyway, Holler is the leader, and Holler wouldn't lift a hoof to save Echo. . . . He tried to have him killed in the first place. . . .

She turned and found the herd staring at her. Holler and his hangers-on were standing where they had peeled from the rest to confront Fearsome, and their gazes were filled with uniform distrust and loathing. Except for one—Tremble was also there, the female who'd followed from the outskirts of the herd. Tremble's eyes were shining with amazement, and she gave Whisper a tiny nod of encouragement, then turned to look behind her at the rest of the herd.

Behind them, the herd was spreading out, releasing the calves and the elderly from the protective circle. And all of them were muttering to one another, staring at Whisper,

EAST MOLINE PUBLIC LIBRARY

shaking their heads. Whisper's heart jolted as she heard snatches of conversation. . . .

"We cannot just abandon him."

"Echo is our rightful leader!"

"What about the migration?"

"There is no migration without a true leader. . . ."

One of the elderly buffalo was pushing her way out of the crowd, and as Whisper drew close to Holler and Tremble, she reached them too. Her movements were a little stiff, but she had a regal bearing that Whisper recognized.

It was Trudge. She was Holler and Bellow's mother, Quake's grandmother. Whisper didn't know her well, but she knew she was wise, and the herd usually listened to her advice. Whisper's breath caught as Trudge approached her son. What would she say?

Please, Trudge, help me. . . . Help Echo. . . .

"That was the wrong decision, my son," she said.

Holler rounded on her, his temper flaring. "I am the leader here!" he bellowed. "Remember your place!"

There was an intake of breath among the herd—especially the females. Trudge drew herself up a little but didn't reprimand her son. She stared him down, though he was a head taller than her even without his enormous horns.

"Echo is our rightful leader," she said. "You risk his life by turning the lion away so rashly."

"What would you have me do then, wise one?" Holler sneered. "Turn three of the herd over to those killers?"

"You turned Echo over to the hyenas," Whisper muttered.

Holler fixed her with a look that made her stomach churn. He looked like he would have liked to spear her on one of his horns right here and now.

"It doesn't matter now," said another voice. Quake had hurried up to his father's side and was addressing his grandmother—with more respect than his father had and a slight tremor in his voice. "Isn't it more important that the migration carries on? Don't we need to keep moving?"

"The migration will fail without Echo," put in Tremble. "Some of us . . ." She stopped, as if a thought had occurred to her. "Some of us would give our lives freely for this cause," she finished softly.

Whisper looked up at her. "That's right," she said. She cleared her throat, tried to speak clearly and loudly, although her heart was pounding and a terrible sadness was rushing over her. "I will go to the lions. I will offer myself in exchange for my brother. It's only right."

A moment of stunned, bleak silence followed.

"I will go too," said Tremble. "I believe in this cause. I believe that without it this migration is doomed to fail." She pushed past Holler, with a roughness that made Whisper gasp, and came to stand beside her. Whisper looked up at the female, hope and gratitude and a deep, deep terror shining in her eyes.

"Thank you," she whispered.

Trudge made an amused *hm* sound under her breath and then slowly made her way over to join them. Whisper stared at her, her mouth falling open.

"I will go with them," said the elderly buffalo.

"No!" Quake gasped. "You can't!"

Trudge blinked fondly at her grandson. "My time is almost at hand. This migration will be my last—if I even return to the dry grazing lands," she said. "I would prefer to give my life in service of something greater than to fall victim to the dangers of the journey. Do not grieve for me, little one."

"No," Quake said again, trembling, pawing the ground with one hoof in distress.

Trudge looked up at her son. Holler met his mother's eyes steadily.

"So be it then," he said at last. "If you're all mad enough to go on this fool's errand, I won't stand in your way. Send the calf Echo back to us if you can. But we won't wait for you. The migration must move on."

"So be it." Trudge nodded. "Come, let's hurry," she said to Whisper and Tremble. "If we hold to our courage and our love for our herd, we can set this right before it is too late. Lead the way, young buffalo."

On shaking hooves, Whisper turned and set out, following after Fearsome.

9

Breathstealer paused for a moment, sniffing her paws and pretending to check they were still going the right way. Why, she wasn't sure—it wasn't as if Graypelt could actually see her.

What am I doing? This is foolishness.

Her last moments in the clan kept coming back to her, new terrible details standing out every time. Gutripper turning her back, not just banishing her daughter but essentially declaring her to be dead. Skullcracker's and Hidetearer's mocking voices following her as she left. The knowledge in her gut that they would kill and eat her—then the blazing relief as Nosebiter appeared and *killed* Skullcracker to save Breathstealer's life.

The things Nosebiter had said then. . . .

One last thing for my sister. The very last.

Now I never want to see you again.

Run, Cub. Run far, far away.

They would not welcome her back, no matter what she said she had seen in her visions.

But she couldn't make herself ignore the vision, so there was nothing else for it.

"So your mother is the leader of your clan," said Graypelt as they pressed on. "What was that like? My mother and father were equals in our pack, with a few other adults and their cubs. Were there a lot of expectations of you?"

Breathstealer let out a bitter laugh. "Maybe for the first month of my life. But not really, no. My older sister has always been the better daughter, and I . . . I had these visions. I never fit in. No, nobody expected anything from me. And I proved them right," she muttered.

"I don't think that can be true," Graypelt said. "What about your sister? Did you get along with her?"

"Yes," Breathstealer said. "Better, anyway. At least, I used to. She saved my life before I left . . . but she also said she never wanted to see me again."

"Do they often throw hyenas out?" Graypelt asked. "I hope you don't mind me asking. Other creatures fascinate me."

"Not often, no." Breathstealer sighed. "I wasn't really expecting it. I thought I'd be punished. Maybe I'd have to stay with the males. . . ."

Graypelt's ears twitched, and Breathstealer began to explain about the males of her clan, how they weren't really full hyenas, how they didn't have real names, just ones they gave themselves, but they still lived with the rest of the clan. . . . She could tell the wolf wasn't really following it all.

"Anyway," she said, "there are punishments and challenges, but they're up to the leader mostly."

"That all sounds rather complicated," Graypelt said, and Breathstealer wondered if he was being politer than he felt. "Tell me . . . do you think your mother believes your visions are real?"

"I don't think she cares," Breathstealer said. "I think she believes either I'm a freak who talks to insects, or I'm a fantasist who makes things up for the attention—either way, best to ignore it and hope it goes away," she added bitterly.

They were coming to the top of a familiar hill now, and as they crested it, the huge baobab tree came into view ahead. She heard a peal of laughter in the distance, and it sounded like home and made her skin crawl, all at once.

"We're nearly there," she said. "I think you shouldn't come with me—not all the way to the clan. They don't like strangers."

"I think you might be right," said Graypelt. Breathstealer's heart sank, even though she knew she *was* right. She would miss his company—and she thought he might well come to a hard end out here on his own. Had she indirectly killed her friend by insisting on taking him out of his jungle?

"Before you go," Graypelt said, "let me give you a little advice. Visions are all very well . . . as a guide. As information. But my understanding is that whatever insight they give you, the really important thing is what *you choose* to do. I think you found that out in my jungle, right? No matter what you're being offered, it has to be a free choice, and if it's not, then I would tread very carefully, because you may not have all the information you need."

"I suppose so," Breathstealer said. She wasn't quite following. She had told Graypelt a bit more about her experience in the bog with the Great Devourer. Did he think she shouldn't listen to her visions? Did he think she shouldn't try to save her *mother*?

He was right about choices, she supposed. But he was a very strange wolf, that was for sure.

"Good luck, Breathstealer," said Graypelt. "May the Great Spirit protect you."

"And you too," said Breathstealer.

The wolf gave her a dignified bow, turned around, and padded away with his oddly careful gait, scenting all the time and dragging his claws through the thin grass before putting his paw down. Breathstealer watched him go for a moment and then turned herself and faced the baobab.

It was time to go home and find out if Gutripper would accept her advice, even to save her own life. . . .

The scent of hyena on the plain around the baobab was so strong, it almost made Breathstealer's head spin. She barely used to notice it, and it had been days since she left, no more. Had her nose forgotten what it was like to live here already?

It wasn't long before she heard yipping shouts and saw a pack of hyenas loping toward her.

"Stop!" one cried. "What are you doing here? This isn't your clan!"

She'd been recognized as an outsider, then. She drew

herself up and tried to look as dignified, and as not-scared, as she could. It helped that she realized all these hyenas were males. They might have greater status than her in the clan now, technically, but just smelling them gave her confidence. She was still naturally their superior, and they would bow to her dominance.

She hoped.

"I am here to speak to Gutripper," she said. "Tell her there is news she will want to hear."

For a moment, the males eyed her with nervy suspicion, then one chuckled.

"Do you think we don't know you, Tailgrabber?" he sneered.

"My name," she said, "is Breathstealer now. I took it for myself, with my claws and my teeth. Keep getting in my way if you want to find out how."

"We'll tell them you're here," one giggled. "But you might not want to be still here when they arrive."

He rushed off, loping at a sprint toward the great tree. Breathstealer tried to keep her face impassive, her ears pricked. She didn't meet the males' eyes and looked up only when she heard more running paws returning.

When she did look, her heart sank, and she almost cowered.

Hidetearer was leading two other hyenas toward her. The others were Throatpiercer and Ribsmasher, two hyenas that Breathstealer barely exchanged two words with while she was still with the clan. She watched, feeling the absence of Skullcracker, who would have accompanied Hidetearer if she'd been alive. She wondered if Hidetearer was feeling it too.

"What's this? Some nameless thing?" Hidetearer growled as they came closer. "Get it off our territory at once."

"I am Breathstealer, and I have come to speak to Gutripper," Breathstealer said again. It was harder to keep her voice even in front of these three. "I have news she needs to hear."

"It's a filthy nameless trick," snarled Ribsmasher. "*Namestealer.*"

Breathstealer's hackles rose, but she managed to swallow her growl. She could argue about her name until the stars fell out of the sky; these hyenas wouldn't accept it, and she didn't need them to.

"Tail— *Cub?*" said a voice, and the male hyenas scuttled out of the way as Nosebiter approached, a limp meerkat dangling from her jaws. Breathstealer met her eyes, hoping for some hint that she was happy to see her sister, or if not happy, then at least willing to listen. Nosebiter's ears twitched, and she dropped her prey at her paws.

"I thought I told you to go," she said. "And never return. What are you doing?"

"I have something I need to tell Gutripper," Breathstealer said once again. Nosebiter would believe her, right?

"Tell me," said Nosebiter flatly.

"It figures you'd listen to her," muttered Hidetearer, rolling her eyes. Nosebiter turned on her, baring her bloodied teeth.

"What did you say to me? Are you challenging my loyalty to the clan, Hidetearer?"

There was a frozen moment when the two faced off, hackles

raised, the others all leaning away from them just a little.

"No," said Hidetearer. "Let's hear the traitor's story." Very slowly, the hyenas all began to relax. "Make it good, name-stealer. It might be your last one."

"I bet she had a *vision*," said Throatpiercer in a mocking voice.

Nosebiter turned a harsh glare on Breathstealer. "Well?"

"I did," said Breathstealer.

The other three females spat, rolled their eyes, and stopped listening, but Breathstealer held Nosebiter's gaze.

"I saw fire around the baobab tree," she said. "I saw Gutripper's den blazing with it. She was inside, trapped and burning. I heard her screams. I know not all of you believe what I see is real," she added. "And perhaps none of you would lift a paw to help me if I was on fire right now. But *I* needed to warn you. Gutripper is in danger."

To her surprise, instead of instant dismissal and more threats, there was a heavy pause. Nosebiter seemed to be thinking hard, and there was a flicker of something new in Hidetearer's eyes. She glanced at Throatpiercer, and something passed between them, though Breathstealer couldn't tell what it was.

"I know you," said Nosebiter at last. "You are no sister, no clan member of ours. But you mean our clan no harm by coming here. You may approach Gutripper and tell her your story, and when she sends you away, you can feel like you've done your duty."

"All right," said Breathstealer. "That's fair."

Hidetearer, Throatpiercer, and Ribsmasher all looked irritated, but none of them challenged Nosebiter. She gave a toss of her head and turned to head toward the tree, and Breathstealer fell in line with her.

"I wouldn't have come if I wasn't really worried—" she began.

"Don't," said Nosebiter under her breath. "You never knew when to stop, Tailgrabber."

Breathstealer's heart gave a strange lurch to hear her old name—it was insulting, but in Nosebiter's voice it suddenly felt like a kindness.

They skirted the baobab's giant trunk and came in sight of her mother's den. There was no sign of fire, no smoke blackening the trunk. And why would it? When fire came, it came when the sky was growling and angry. Yet the sky was clear today.

Gutripper herself was just visible within the den. Breathstealer hesitated, and Nosebiter went ahead, speaking to their mother in a low voice. Breathstealer saw the moment when Nosebiter broke the news that she had returned—Gutripper's ears pricked up, and she shot a furious look in her direction.

But a moment later, Nosebiter gestured with her tail, and Breathstealer approached the den. She kept her head respectfully bowed, not that she thought it would mean much to Gutripper—which meant she was almost standing right in front of her mother when she looked up and saw why she was inside the den instead of out on the plain. Gutripper's back leg was swollen and red beneath the fur, and her paw looked like it wasn't lying at the angle it should be.

"Take a good look, Cub," said her mother. "This is the reason I haven't chased you from our territory myself, and instead I'm forced to accept Nosebiter's questionable decision-making. Tell me your story, before I make a different decision."

Breathstealer nodded. *It's also the reason you're in danger*, she thought. But it wouldn't help to start that way with her mother. She took a deep breath and launched into a description of her vision—more detailed than what she had given the others, wringing every drop of fear and portent from it she could.

Gutripper listened with a curled lip. "Your vision is telling you I am immobile. *Vulnerable*," she said once Breathstealer was finished. "I think you risked your life to tell me something I very much already know. Take her away, Nosebiter, I don't want to look at her anymore."

"Come on," her sister hissed.

Breathstealer let Nosebiter lead her away, and waited until she thought they were out of Gutripper's earshot before she frowned.

"I don't think that's it," she said urgently. "It *could* be, but I don't think so. There's got to be something else."

Nosebiter shook her head.

"You can stay in the dens for tonight," she said. "In the morning, you go. Don't speak to me. It'll be too hard. For you," she added quickly, and unconvincingly.

Then she turned and walked away, leaving Breathstealer alone to curl up in the roots of the baobab for one more night.

Am I wrong? Have I really come here for nothing?

Suddenly a thought occurred to her that made her shiver: *What if the vision was false? What if the Great Devourer was punishing me for running? What if it thought the clan would kill me?*

Well . . . if that was true, then the Great Devourer had been wrong. Her family might no longer recognize her as family, but here she was, safe for the night, tolerated, maybe even believed.

There were much worse ways to spend the night.

10

The scent of buffalo was strong, but Stride frowned as he sniffed at a pile of dung and then looked around. There was something strange about the trail. It was as if the buffalo herd had been going in circles, layering their own scents on top of themselves as they went.

"I smell death," muttered Stonehide. "A buffalo?"

"There's certainly something," said Stride. He could see a crowd of vultures flapping around something behind a big rock. As they drew closer, he heard voices speaking grass-tongue, and he hung back to peer cautiously around the rock.

It was indeed a buffalo. Probably an old one that had been too tired to carry on the journey. There were three hyenas with their muzzles buried deep in one side and a flock of vultures pecking at the other—the corpse was so large that an uneasy peace had broken out between the two groups of scavengers.

Stonehide marched out from behind the rock. "Any of you fine fellows seen the herd this one came from? Which way did they go?"

The hyenas looked up and chuckled. Two of them went straight back to eating, but the third licked her lips and nodded with her bloodied muzzle across the plain toward a shallow valley, its lower slopes wreathed in mist. "They've gone that way, but they won't get far. This migration of theirs isn't going very well for them."

"All the better for you, eh?" Stonehide said.

The hyena chuckled again. "They've barely gone a day or two from their big spiky hill, and three of the old ones have dropped dead. It's feasting time for us and our flapping friends here. There's plenty to go around if you want to get in," she added. "No need to fight for it."

"Their special leader fell off a cliff," said one of the other hyenas, her mouth full of buffalo meat, so that Stride wasn't sure she'd really said it. She swallowed and nodded. "I think that's what happened, anyway. That was Gutripper's lot, but word travels. Some special calf who was supposed to lead them on the migration got chased off a cliff near here."

"Now they're going round in circles," sniggered the third hyena, "so I guess he must have been the best at directions after all."

Stride met Stonehide's eyes and nodded.

"Where's the cliff?" he asked the hyenas.

"Opposite direction to the valley," said one. "Go up that rise, look for the trees that look like a pair of giraffes having a fight, then follow the setting sun. It's a big old ravine, you can't miss it."

"Nor could the buffalo calf," said another hyena, and they all burst into cackling laughter.

Sure enough, they found the two fighting-giraffe trees, tall and nearly bare trunks intertwined, and between them the setting sun illuminated the view of a gradually sloping plain that was suddenly cut off by the edge of a deep ravine dotted with rocks and trees.

"I don't know why," Stride muttered as they made their way toward the cliff, "but I'm surprised they gave us the right directions. I never liked hyenas. There's just something about them. They're *weird*."

"Well, they eat rot-meat—although when times are tough, you eat what you can get," said Stonehide. "And there's all the laughing obviously. I reckon they're all a bit mad. No wonder they still follow the Great Devourer."

"Do they?" Stride's fur prickled. "All of them?"

"I don't know about *all*. The story I heard at my mother's teat said that they used to live in a kingdom all underground and serve the Devourer before the Great Spirit brought light to Bravelands. Something like that."

"Underground . . . ," Stride muttered. "The Great Devourer lives underground?"

"In the stories," said Stonehide slowly, casting a sideways glance at Stride. "Makes sense. That's where bodies go, if you leave 'em long enough."

"And spirits?"

"I suppose, before the Great Spirit takes them to the stars. Maybe."

"And this underground place. If hyenas lived there, there must be a way to get there."

Stonehide stopped walking. "I'm sure there would be," he said, "if it was real. It's a story, mate. And a creepy one at that. I don't think there was really a time when the moon was eaten by a honey badger either. Although I'd like to meet the badger that did it," he added with a chuckle.

I don't know, thought Stride. *I saw Flicker dragged down into the ground. The Great Mother thinks spirits are going missing. A cheetah stole the sun from Death, and now Death chases cheetahs who run too fast. I know that's true. Why not the rest?*

He shook himself as they approached the cliff edge. He had to focus here, or he might find himself facing the same fate as Echo. He sniffed along the cliff until he caught it: a mingled scent of buffalo and hyena. They had both passed this way, but the smell was weak. He peered down and saw a well-trodden path that looked like it could support passing buffalo, though he couldn't see how to get to it other than climbing down the cliff itself. Luckily, it wasn't too challenging, with plenty of little ledges big enough for him to balance on. He stepped down onto the first one, testing its strength under his paws. It seemed fine.

"Come on," he said to Stonehide. "It's a short leopard-hop down here to the place the buffalo go."

Stonehide didn't respond at first. Stride looked around and found the honey badger grimacing over the edge of the cliff.

"If I can fit, you can," Stride said. "Just follow me."

"*Hrmm*," said Stonehide.

"Oh." Stride couldn't help a sly grin passing over his face. "Have we finally found something the fearsome Stonehide is afraid of?"

"No," Stonehide said quickly. "Not afraid. I've just got short legs for some of those drops, is all. You go on, though, my leggy pal, I'll find my way."

"All right," said Stride. "Shout if you get stuck." And with that he began to climb down, balancing on thin ledges and leaping little gaps, digging his claws in when rock turned to earth and thin, spiky grasses. He paused every so often, pretending to catch his breath and waiting for Stonehide, in case he needed help. The honey badger was struggling down after him on trembling paws, snorting and cursing under his breath. Despite fitting easily onto the ledges, his short legs didn't seem to have the same ability to balance as Stride's longer ones.

"Don't topple over," Stride said. "I don't want to have to try to catch you."

Stonehide growled. "Well, I don't want to have to pull your entrails out, so a bit of quiet, please."

Stride smirked but stayed quiet until they finally reached the ground. He busied himself with sniffing around, and by

the time Stonehide had clambered down onto the flat path
and caught his breath Stride could tell that hyenas and buffalo had trampled off the path, out onto a jutting rock. He
stood at the edge of the rock and looked down into the river
below. The muddy brown water didn't look all that deep, but
it was impossible to tell. There could be powerful currents
underneath.

"If he fell in there, he *might* have survived . . . ," he muttered
when Stonehide joined him. "But he must have *looked* like he'd
sunk, or the other buffalo would know he was still alive."

Stonehide peered up and down the line of the river. "A big
buffalo could swim against that current, but maybe a little one
would struggle. And we can't follow on the bank on this side,
the cliffs go right to the water there. We'll have to cross over
if we want to get downriver."

He was right. They had to get across. "I guess we're lucky
that it hasn't rained in so long. We can probably swim across.
Actually . . ." He squinted. "There's a little mud island right
there. I bet I can jump it, if I land there." He turned to Stonehide. "Do you think I can make it across without getting a
paw wet?"

"No," said Stonehide. "But please, do try."

They made their way back through the bushes to the path
and then down to the edge of the water. Stride stretched out
his back and wiggled his tail, fixing his gaze on the wet gray
muddy patch in the middle of the stream. On the other side
there was a slippery-looking but definitely climbable bank. If
he kept his momentum up, he'd probably be able to get up to

solid ground without falling back into the water.

"See you on the other side," said Stonehide, slipping into the river and beginning to swim across with strong, sure paddles of his short legs. Stride grinned, took a little run up, and launched himself at the gray muddy island. . . .

Which tilted under his paws the moment they touched down. The mud was not mud. It was soft, squashy skin. Horror gripped Stride as he realized his mistake, and then he was plunged into the river. In the silty water he saw the creature turn its head to glare at him, opening its jaws to show off tusks as long as his arm.

Writhing and kicking desperately, Stride panicked his way through the water, somehow making it to land before the hippopotamus chomped him in half. He scrambled his way up onto the bank, gasping and slipping, shot up onto a rock, and stood there, dripping miserably and shaking.

Stonehide was sitting on the bank, cleaning his wet fur with a long tongue.

"Don't topple over," he muttered. "You might get a paw wet."

The hippo emerged from the water, not quite charging, but blowing out furious steam from its nostrils.

"*Excuse* me," it bellowed, stomping toward them.

"I'm sorry!" Stride yelped.

"Please, forgive my stupid friend," said Stonehide. "May I ask you a question about a buffalo?"

Stride watched in stunned amazement as his honey badger friend absolutely befuddled yet another creature. This time it was the polite manner and utter lack of fear that stopped the hippo in its tracks, not his surprising strength or wild aggression, but the effect was the same.

"Um," said the hippo. "I suppose so. . . ."

"Thank you, thank you very much," said Stonehide. "We heard that there was a buffalo calf who fell into this river here and drowned. Have you seen a buffalo calf passing by?"

"No," said the hippo thoughtfully. "But I've seen a lot of those little birds that follow the buffalo around."

"Oxpeckers?" said Stonehide.

The hippo bobbed his giant head. "They were swarming a little farther down, that way." He gave his snout another sway.

"Thank you so much," said Stonehide with a little bow, which Stride thought was laying it on a bit thick. But the hippo seemed to appreciate it. He glared up at Stride and grunted.

"Be more careful next time," he grumbled and slid backward into the water, sinking until only his round back and his eyes were poking up above the surface.

"Come on," Stonehide muttered out of the corner of his mouth. "Let's go."

Stride didn't need telling twice.

They hurried along the bank, Stride stopping a few times to shake the water from his fur. He peered up into the sky, searching for little birds, and then he almost stumbled over his paws as his nose picked up a sudden strong scent of buffalo.

"Where is it?" he muttered. He sniffed the ground and the air, but the smell seemed as if it was coming from the river.

He drew closer to the water, opening his mouth and closing his eyes. It was . . .

"There!" said Stonehide. "See that branch?"

Stride opened his eyes and saw it. A big fallen branch, beached on the edge of the river, and on the branch was a big clump of hair.

"Buffalo hair, definitely," Stride said, sniffing at it. "It was here. And it was . . ." He sniffed deeper, feeling the hair tickling his nose. "I think it was scared. Which means it was alive!"

"Stride, look," said Stonehide. He had climbed up the bank a little way, clinging to a rock in a way that made Stride tilt his head in confusion. Why wouldn't he just walk on the sandy earth—

Oh. Because there's a hoofprint there!

"It went this way," Stonehide said, a raspy triumph in his voice. "And when it did, it was walking. We're on the right track."

11

The three buffalo walked in silence. Whisper wished that one of the others would say something, but there was nothing that could make this moment less bleak. She guessed they were both lost in their own thoughts, of family and friends they would leave behind, things they would never see again, never do. The sun was setting.

I may never see the dawn.

Whisper felt like she was fighting to keep her head above water, against a rising tide of emotion. She was buffeted by thoughts of Bellow and Thunder, while the question of Echo's fate weighed her down like a stomach full of stones. What if she gave her life, and it didn't even save him?

Suddenly she heard a scuffling sound, above the slow march of their hoofsteps, and she spun around. Another buffalo was galloping across the plain toward them.

It was Quake.

"Wait," he was calling. "Stop, wait!"

Whisper's mind whirled as the others paused and turned to look. What did Quake want? Why would he risk his life, coming so far from the herd all alone?

It couldn't be . . . he wasn't planning to give himself up . . . ?

"What are you after?" she asked as he stopped and stood panting near them. "Are you . . . coming with us?"

"No!" Quake gasped. "No way. And nor are you. None of you. This is foolishness."

"Maybe," Whisper said, "but I cannot give up on Echo. Not again."

"You can't trust the lions," Quake insisted.

"I can't trust *you*," Whisper spat. "You're just here to stop us because Holler doesn't want Echo alive."

"That's not true," Quake said. "My father told me not to come, he—" Quake broke off. "Grandmother." He appealed to Trudge, his eyes shining in the golden light. "They might not even *have* Echo. You're all going to die for nothing!"

Trudge shook her head sadly. "Not at all, dear. Please, go home."

"Yes," Whisper growled under her breath. "Run back to Daddy."

Quake didn't leave. He stared miserably as they turned their backs on him and walked on. Whisper thought she should probably feel bad that her last interaction with him might be a cruel and pointless jibe. But she didn't.

Her stomach lurched painfully as they drew closer to the

lion den. They were there waiting for the buffalo, she could smell them.

"Courage, you two," said Trudge. "Echo needs us now."

Whisper was grateful for the words, especially since her own throat had closed up and she couldn't seem to make a sound.

Tremble was the first to step out around the corner of the overhang and expose herself to the view of the lions there. Whisper followed, and the sight chilled her blood. There were so many. A male with a giant bushy mane—Noble, she remembered—sat staring at them, his paws crossed and an expression of satisfaction on his face. Around him, six females and three more young males were all watching the buffalo with naked hunger in their eyes. Whisper's legs trembled with the urge to run, her heart picking up speed. Every instinct she had was screaming at her.

Death. This is death. You have to run. Find the herd. Run!

There was no sign of Echo, so Whisper planted her hooves in the dust and forced herself to stand still.

"Well, spirit bless my paws," said Fearsome, standing up. "The calf followed through. I told you I thought she would, didn't I, Savage?"

"Yes, yes," said another female, with a sarcastic smile. "You were right and I was wrong. I guess the runt must really be special."

"Where is Echo?" Whisper rasped.

The lions looked up at their pride leader. Noble nodded without a word, and Savage stood up and headed into the trees. She didn't go far. Something raised itself from the undergrowth and walked unsteadily, almost like a newborn calf, out into the harsh sunset glare.

It *was* Echo.

Whisper's heart soared at the sight of her little brother, even though he looked awful: there was a claw-gash on his flank, he was limping, and he cringed away from Savage in terror, glassy eyes not focusing on anything. He looked as if he had been tossed around by fate and had barely come out in one piece. He looked so small. She had almost forgotten how small he really was.

But then he looked up, and his eyes met hers, and Whisper's heart swelled until it ached as his expression brightened. His tail began to swish in excited circles.

"Whisper," he said, his voice a hoarse gasp. "It's you! You're here!"

"I'm here," she replied, her eyes filling with tears. "It's going to be okay, Echo. I'm going to get you out of here."

Echo was staring from her to the bigger buffalo, hope burning in his eyes. Whisper's whole body went cold.

"Listen to me, Echo," she said. "When—when you leave here, you need to find the oxpeckers and find Bellow. He's with Thunder. He can tell you everything you need to know. You'll be a good leader, Echo, I know you will. And I'll always be with you."

"What . . ." Echo didn't understand. How could he? "Of course you will. . . . We're leaving. . . ."

"You're leaving," Whisper said with a bleak and desperate

smile. "I made a promise, and I think Noblepride expects me to keep it."

The lions were getting up, licking their muzzles. Echo started to shake his head. "I don't understand."

But his eyes told her that he did.

"Are you really willing to give your lives for this creature?" Fearsome asked.

"We are," said Tremble.

The lions began to slowly circle the buffalo, Savage standing still by Echo's side. Once again, Whisper had to fight every instinct to stand there and let the predators get behind her.

"You'll be all right, Echo," Whisper babbled. "Remember everything I've told you. Don't be scared."

"Stop it," Echo said. "Why are you talking like this? I can't go back without you! I need you!"

Whisper swallowed. Her voice shook. "You'll be wonderful," she said. "You don't need me. You need to go, now!"

"No!"

"Well, isn't this touching," said Noble, the pride leader. He spoke with a deep, soft tone that might have been almost soothing, if it hadn't been for the drool collecting in the corner of his mouth and the way he ran his large red tongue over his fangs. "I have good news for you both. You won't have to live without each other."

"What?" growled Tremble.

"Did you think we would let this tasty morsel leave?" said Noble. Savage was suddenly on the other side of Echo, preventing him from leaving the circle of the den. She growled and licked her lips. Echo squeaked in fear and stumbled back, but he had nowhere to go.

"No! We had a deal!" Whisper gasped.

"Lions don't make deals with grass-eaters," spat Fearsome. "Lions take what they want."

"Buffalo honor their word," said Trudge. She stomped forward, shouldering Whisper aside so that her back was against the rock. "And on my word, you will regret your dishonesty."

"Enough," said Noble, and at the same time Trudge swung her head to Whisper and muttered,

"Get Echo. Run. Don't look back."

"Eat your fill, Noblepride!" Noble roared.

Tremble reared up on her back legs, kicked her front hooves in the air, and charged him with a bellowing cry. The lion ducked out of the way just in time, but Tremble barreled past him and into one of the lionesses who had not been as fast, throwing her into the air with a toss of her horns.

There was a yowl of pain and a chorus of hissing and spitting as Trudge kicked out with her back legs, catching one of the lions who'd tried to creep up behind them.

Whisper sucked in a breath and let it out in a furious yell as she put her head down and charged toward Echo and Savage. The lioness was looking at Echo, preparing to pounce, and when she saw Whisper coming her eyes went wide and dark for a second before Whisper's half-formed horns struck her in the side. She didn't have the strength to lift and toss the lion like Tremble had, but she felt something inside the lion snap, and then Savage was sprawled on the ground, gasping for breath and yowling furiously.

"Whisper!" Echo said, and thumped his head against hers. "We have to get out!"

"Into the trees," Whisper said. "We're small enough, we can make it."

But she couldn't help turning back to look at the others, hesitating. *Should* they run? Three of the lions were down and groaning already, and one more was not moving. What if she stayed and fought? What if Trudge and Tremble could beat them with her help?

But then Echo let out a startled cry, and Whisper stumbled as a heavy weight landed on her back. She reared, and pain jolted between her shoulders. One of the young males had jumped on her, biting down, just missing her neck. She gave a panicked leap and threw herself backward against the closest tree trunk, once, twice. The lion's claws dug in deeper, but on the third swing it lost its grip with a tearing of flesh and hair and went flying into a bush.

And Tremble and Trudge were struggling now. Noble had his jaws locked around Tremble's front leg. Fearsome and two other lions were piled on Trudge's back, holding on despite her weakening thrashes.

"Go! Run!" Tremble yelled.

"Whisper!" Echo said. "Please!"

It was Echo's voice that got her moving. Echo needed her. He was alive, and he needed her to live too.

They ran into the trees, breaking branches and trampling ferns.

"This way!" cried Quake. He was standing in the shadow of a tree—lurking, seeing what would happen, spying for Holler—but right now, he was better than the lions. They veered toward him, and he led them through a tight squeeze between two tree trunks, and then they were out on the plain again and picking up speed, as much as they could with Echo's stumbling limp slowing him down. Whisper could hear the angry cries and screams of pain following them as they stampeded away, and her heart ached for Tremble and for Trudge.

But she was running beside her little brother. Echo was alive, and they were together, and nothing would tear them apart again.

12

She jolted awake, the scent of smoke in her muzzle, her mother's cries echoing in her ears. Breathstealer scrambled from the den out into the night and spun a tight circle in the darkness, looking for the red flicker of flames.

There was nothing. The night was cool. The sky overhead was the deep gray of approaching dawn, speckled with fading stars. No smoke, no screams.

She heard snuffles and snores from nearby. She had been given a den right on the edge of the male side of the tree, not quite with them, not quite apart. Nothing seemed to have roused them.

It was just a dream. There had been no insects, just her mind turning the vision over and over. It probably didn't mean anything.

But anxiety twitched in Breathstealer's paws.

I have to check. She won't thank me. She might do a lot worse than yell at me. But I can't just go back to sleep.

She padded around the edge of the tree, careful not to step on any of the hyenas who lay sprawled and snoring nearby. She would poke her nose into Gutripper's den, make sure she was sleeping soundly, she wouldn't wake her. Maybe she would stand guard until the rest of the clan woke. Just in case . . .

Suddenly Breathstealer stopped in her tracks, holding her paw in front of her. Something had moved. In the predawn light, there was a patch of gray, a flitting shadow, moving from tree to rock just barely within eyesight. She stared out at the shape, her breath coming faster. Was it a lion? Had she somehow brought a lion here . . . *again?*

But no . . . as she watched, the shape paused and looked up, sniffing the air, its pointed ears and skinny frame freezing for a moment before it vanished behind another rock.

Graypelt!

What was he doing here? She'd told him to stay away. Had he got turned around, unable to see where he was going? Had he wandered into their territory by mistake? *Surely* he would smell the scents of the hyenas. . . .

He didn't seem to be coming any closer. In fact, just as Breathstealer was thinking of running over there and trying to explain to him that he needed to leave, she saw him emerge from behind his rock, turn, and make his way up the gentle slope to the top of the hill they had parted on once more. Soon he was lost in the haze of gray light.

He must have realized where he'd found himself, she thought. *I just hope he goes far away from this place! It's no place for a lone wolf, let alone a blind one.* Something told her that her word would count for little if she tried to defend him.

Shaking herself, she padded on toward Gutripper's den. A hyena was sitting outside the den, and for a moment she thought that it was her mother, recovered enough to sit up. But then the hyena turned to glare at her, and her heart sank. It was Hidetearer.

"I thought you were told to sleep on the other side of the tree," Hidetearer snarled. "Are you lost? Or do you want me to send you back there with a few new scars?"

"I need to see Gutripper," Breathstealer said.

"You do not," Hidetearer said coldly. "Isn't it enough that you've got me standing watch here for no reason?"

Breathstealer tried not to smile. So Gutripper had believed her! At least, Breathstealer's words of warning had made some kind of impact. . . .

"Nobody wants you here, Tailgrabber," Hidetearer sneered. She took a step away from the den's mouth, advancing on Breathstealer with a terrible idea gleaming in her eyes. "Who's to say you didn't come here to kill Gutripper after all? Lucky I was here to stop you. You fought to the last, you basically *forced* me to snap your neck. . . ."

Breathstealer tensed, baring her teeth.

And then an unearthly howl split the air. Breathstealer's body felt cold. It was the same sound she'd heard in her dream. It was the sound of her mother in horrific pain.

She shouldered past Hidetearer, who was looking around

in shock, and ran for the mouth of the den.

It was dark inside. No flames, no smoke—only the high-pitched and terrible howling. Gutripper was curled up near the back of the den, between the roots of the baobab tree, and she was twitching all over. In the dim light, Breathstealer didn't understand what she was seeing: for a moment she thought that Gutripper's skin was moving by itself, her fur crawling over her body, seemingly *biting* her. But then Gutripper roared, mad with agony, and rolled over, and Breathstealer saw something small and dark gripped in her jaws. It was a scorpion.

It was *dozens* of scorpions, all of them swarming over Gutripper, stinging and biting her.

Breathstealer heard the voices of other hyenas outside the den.

"Help!" she howled. "Hidetearer, help!"

She steeled herself and pounced on her mother, biting down on her fur, catching two scorpions in her jaws, crunching them and tossing them aside. She flinched as another one flexed its sting at her, but she forced herself to keep on grabbing at them, stomping and chewing.

There was barely room for both Gutripper and Breathstealer in the den, but Hidetearer managed to squeeze in too. To her credit, she didn't waste time asking what was happening or blaming Breathstealer—she gaped for a moment and gave a horrified gasp of breath, but then she waded in and tore at the scorpions alongside Breathstealer.

All of a sudden, Breathstealer's teeth were closing on

empty fur, and there was an awful scuttling feeling around her paws. The scorpions were running. Outside the den, she heard yelps of surprise and horror as the arachnids streamed past the other hyenas.

"Mother!" Breathstealer gasped. "Are you all right?"

Gutripper turned a furious, pain-maddened glare on her and began to push herself, on three twitching limbs, toward the entrance of the den. Breathstealer and Hidetearer both got out of the way quickly, backing into the noses of the others as they tried to get out. Gutripper managed to drag herself to the mouth of the den.

"Kill them!" she howled. Her jaws were bloody, and she spat shards of scorpion chitin as she spoke. "Kill them!"

Several of the hyenas scampered off at once after the scorpions. Breathstealer stayed with Gutripper. Nosebiter was outside the den too, and her eyes were wide as she looked at the state of their mother.

"What happened?" she gasped. "Hidetearer! You were supposed to be watching!"

"I was!" Hidetearer snarled. "There were a whole pack of the things, I would have seen them!"

"I don't understand," said Gutripper in a small voice. All the hyenas turned to look at her, and Breathstealer felt cold. She had almost never heard her mother's voice sound timid before, but now it was faint and strange.

Then Gutripper slumped again, and her whole body twitched violently. Breathstealer looked for more scorpions, but there were none—she was just shaking. A high-pitched squeal, like a ghostly echo of the scream she had heard in her dreams, emanated from Gutripper's throat.

"Fire!" she gasped. "Burning! It's burning. . . ."

And then she spasmed, one more time, and went completely still.

"Mother?" Nosebiter said.

Gutripper's flanks fell, in a long and terrible exhale, and they didn't rise again.

Silence fell. The sun broke over the ridge of the hill, casting spears of blinding light and thick, dark shadows over the hyenas at the den. For a moment, no hyena moved. Then Nosebiter shook herself, stood, and turned her back on Gutripper's body. Breathstealer joined her, and the rest all followed suit, turning away from the flesh that had once been their leader, where she was no more. Across the dawn-lit plain, she saw hyenas look up, see and understand what had happened, and turn their backs on the baobab tree.

Nosebiter finally broke the silence with a soft howl that made Breathstealer shiver. A respectful hush remained as the hyenas shifted to look at one another. At least, until Hidetearer sneered, "This is all Tailgrabber's fault. . . ."

"Shut up, Hidetearer," said Nosebiter.

"She distracted me and—"

"Shut up, Hidetearer," Nosebiter said again. "Breathstealer tried to warn us. She told us Gutripper was in danger. If we had taken her more seriously, we might have been able to stop this. We should have taken her seriously from the first time she had one of her visions."

Breathstealer's fur twitched with surprise, and a warm feeling began to come over her, like the warmth of the bright sun on her flank. She hadn't even told her sister her new name. She must have asked the males.

Nosebiter cared. She really did.

"What are you saying?" muttered Ribcracker. "That we should let her back into the clan?"

"You're not our leader," growled Hidetearer darkly.

"I said what I said," Nosebiter replied.

Breathstealer found her gaze drawn out to the grass beyond the tree roots. Hyenas were stalking through it now, sniffing at the ground, occasionally pouncing—but coming up empty-jawed. The scorpions seemed to have vanished.

But where had they come from? And would they be back?

EAST MOLINE PUBLIC LIBRARY

13

They were getting close, Stride was certain of it. The buffalo tracks had vanished in a confusion of older and newer hoofprints, but the scent was strong. They were approaching a small patch of trees. The calf had come this way. There had been lions. It had been afraid. . . .

He raised his head, his nose picking up a fresh stink of frightened buffalo on the wind, a sliver of a moment before he heard the thunder. Hoofbeats, fast and coming closer. He looked at Stonehide, who crouched warily, and then the undergrowth exploded into shards of twig and leaf as three big buffalo burst out of the forest.

Small buffalo, he reminded himself a little hysterically. *These monsters are just calves!*

The smallest buffalo let out a frightened squeal at the sight of Stride and Stonehide in their path, but the middle-size one

114

EAST MOLINE PUBLIC LIBRARY

nudged him a little, and they simply veered aside and stampeded past. Stride was about to call out Echo's name—surely, one of these calves had to be the missing one—but he swallowed his cry as he heard and smelled their pursuers. Pulled along in their wake like dust, three lions roared and slobbered and ignored Stride completely in their frantic chase.

Stride took a step to follow, looked at Stonehide.

"Go!" Stonehide barked, and Stride took off. He felt a strange burst of joy as he approached full speed, like a bird diving from a tall tree, as if he simply had to let go and his legs would do what they were made to do.

He soon caught up with the lions and the buffalo, running alongside, catching angry glances from the lions and terrified ones from their prey. If he could just speak to the buffalo, maybe help steer them away . . . but there was no way to get their attention. The lions were herding the buffalo toward a rock ridge, and Stride abruptly slowed as he realized they were going to be trapped. Sure enough, the buffalo realized too late that they had to turn back and clattered to a stop alongside the ridge. The lions crowded them, growling, all six creatures panting from the chase.

"Wait!" one of the buffalo, the biggest one, called out. "I'm not involved in this! My father is the leader of the herd, if you kill me there'll be trouble!"

The middle-size buffalo gave him a look of pure hatred.

"What do we care?" snarled a lion.

Another lion turned on Stride as he ran up. "Back off, cheetah, this is our prey."

The buffalo were casting their heads this way and that.

"Great Mother Starlight sent me to find this buffalo calf," said Stride, trying to sound confident, all the while trying to put himself between the three massive creatures who could break his bones with a sneeze and the three hungry, angry predators who'd take pleasure in ripping him apart. "In the name of the Great Spirit, you must release these buffalo to me."

The lions were silent for a moment, looking at one another as though considering his declaration. Maybe this would be easier than he thought. . . .

They all burst out laughing.

"Because he is the *chosen one*, I suppose," one yowled sarcastically.

Stride tried not to look surprised. *They know? And they plan to eat him anyway?*

Ugh. Lions.

"I have orders from the Great Mother to protect the calf," Stride said again. "Think hard before you hurt him."

"Our pride does not answer to the Spirit," growled one of the lions. She sniffed dismissively. "And we certainly do not answer to whatever nonsense beliefs these overgrown cows have. Or skinny cheetahs. Lions answer to no one!"

Stride tensed, his stomach tightening. Could he fight off three lions? Of course not. They'd break his neck like a twig. He could see Stonehide catching up now, but even with the hardy, angry little badger's help, could he really survive this fight?

One of the lions scented Stonehide's approach and turned her head to look. She startled, much more violently than

Stride expected. Maybe they had faced honey badgers before and learned their lesson. . . .

But it seemed it was more than that. The lion drew closer to the one who had sniffed at him, her paws dancing anxiously in the dust.

"Fearsome!" she hissed. "Fearsome! It's *him!*"

The lion Fearsome looked around as Stonehide slowed to a saunter. He said nothing, but Fearsome growled at him as if he had insulted her.

"He's back," said the third lion.

"We should tell Noble," said the first.

"Yes, you should," said Stonehide. "Run and tell him now. These buffalo are under my protection."

"This is bigger than a meal," muttered the first lion.

Fearsome fixed Stride and then Stonehide with a furious glare. But then she backed off, dropping her tail and stepping away. The others followed her as she walked off, not running, not looking back. Stonehide watched them retreat with narrowed eyes.

The buffalo watched them go too, breathing hard. When the lions were out of sight, the smallest one spoke up.

"Thank you!" he said. "Did the Great Mother really send you?"

"How did you *do* that?" said the middle-size one, the female, looking down at Stonehide. "It's like you put a spell on them!"

"Lions know not to mess with honey badgers," said Stonehide.

Stride could see in the female's frown that she didn't believe him any more than Stride himself did—but she didn't argue.

"I'm Whisper," she said. "This is Echo. That's Quake," she added with another glare at the bigger calf.

"I'm Stride, and this is Stonehide," said Stride. "Echo—you are the one I was sent to find."

"You were just in time," said Echo, hoarsely.

Stonehide was, Stride thought. *Stonehide is the one who needed to be here. Why didn't Starlight just send him?*

And what did he do to those lions? They knew *him.*

He shook himself, as if he could dislodge some of his questions like irritating fleas.

"You can come with us," Stride said. "We'll escort you back to the Great Mother. You'll be safe there. Come on."

The buffalo exchanged looks. None of them moved.

"I can't," Echo said at last.

"We . . . could," Whisper said slowly. "We could find Bellow, tell him to meet us there . . . if you wanted to go somewhere safe, instead of back to the herd with Holler. . . ."

But the little calf shook his head.

"I can't. I have a duty. I've got to lead the herd."

Stride blinked. It was bizarre to hear such portentous words in the squeaky voice of a cub, but it seemed he meant it, and the bigger female took in his words with a serious expression.

"Then we should get going before those lions come back," she said.

Stride shared a puzzled look with Stonehide. Starlight hadn't actually told him to bring Echo back—just to find him. *And who am I to stand in the way of buffalo business?*

"All right," Stride said. "If you're sure. We won't interfere."

"Thank you again," said Whisper.

"Don't thank us," said Stonehide. "Thank the Great Spirit. It's looking out for you."

"Well, I'm glad it sent you," said Whisper. "Come, Echo. This way."

Stride sat and cleaned his paws as he watched the three buffalo walk away.

"So," he said, "what *did* you do to the lions? Why do they know you?"

"Who said they know me?" Stonehide asked, and got up and started to walk off.

"I think *it's him* was pretty clear," Stride said. He followed after Stonehide, frustration building in his chest. "I think *we need to tell Noble he's back* is a strong indication they knew you."

Stonehide didn't answer for a moment. Then he said, "There's a watering hole there, let's have a drink."

Stride shook his head. "I don't understand you sometimes. You know those lions are going to come back, and I'll find out one way or another!"

Stonehide still didn't answer him. Stride sighed and followed again. Perhaps he just had to give his friend time. He would be quiet and give him space, and maybe then he would open up.

That lasted all the way to the edge of the water, and then Stride just couldn't do it anymore.

"I think Flicker's in trouble," he blurted. "I spoke to the Great Mother. She says something's going on with the Great

Devourer, that maybe it's capturing spirits who should have gone to the stars, and I think that happened to Flicker, and I don't know what to do."

Stonehide remained quiet. Stride was just building up an angry growl, when he noticed the look on Stonehide's face as he gazed over the shallow water. His eyes were wide and dark. His expression had lost all its aggressive humor. He looked almost like a cub.

"Silvertail," he muttered. "She's here."

"*Who?*" said Stride.

"There," whispered Stonehide. Stride looked up, scanning the banks of the watering hole for another honey badger, maybe some other kind of creature, but they were alone for now, apart from a small swarm of butterflies that fluttered past Stonehide's nose.

Stonehide's head whipped around to follow them. Stride watched in confusion, annoyance, and then deep concern as Stonehide took off after the fluttering insects, running around the edge of the water. *Why is he chasing butterflies?* But Stonehide seemed mesmerized, muttering under his breath as he waddled after the insects. They kept ahead of him, no doubt as confused as Stride about this strange pursuer, until they alighted on a splintered tree stump. One by one they crawled into the cavity in the center and vanished. Stonehide arrived a moment later, and immediately attacked the base of the stump, digging. His tough claws raked the earth around the tree, sending out clouds of dust and bits of twig.

"Silvertail, wait for me!" he cried.

Stride just sat and watched him, a sinking feeling in his heart. Was his friend having some kind of vision—or had he just lost his mind? Perhaps he'd taken a blow at some point, or the chase with the buffalo had exhausted him. When should he try to intervene? Stonehide was digging so frantically— he was so in his own world—that Stride almost feared to get close, in case his companion turned on him in his frenzy or even attacked him. Stride might lose an eye!

So he just waited while Stonehide scraped and clawed at the tree stump, reducing it to a pile of old dry wood, until finally his desperate clawing slowed and stopped. He stood there in a heap of splinters, his breathing ragged as he stared at the destruction under his feet. Gradually, his heaving flanks slowed.

"It was her," he said at last. "I'm sure it was." He shook his head, still not meeting Stride's eyes.

"The butterflies?" said Stride, still not understanding.

"You see, I'm sorry to say I know just what you're going through with Flicker," said Stonehide, not answering the question. Stride didn't press him, waiting for the honey badger to speak again.

"My mate, Silvertail. She was killed, eaten by the lions of Noblepride."

"I'm sorry," said Stride. "I had no idea." How this related to the butterflies was still a mystery, but one that could wait.

"Our unborn cubs too," said Stonehide sadly.

Stride swallowed. "That's . . . awful," he said, aware that *awful* was not a sufficient word to encompass what Stonehide had just told him.

"So . . . I took revenge." Stonehide finally turned and fixed Stride with a look so bleak it made Stride shift uncomfortably, backing away just a little. "I killed Noble's mate. That's what made me a Codebreaker. *They* are not Codebreakers, they were hunting to survive. The Great Spirit never said you couldn't be cruel about it. But *I* snuck into their camp in the night and tore out that lion's throat, just so her mate would know a sliver of the pain I felt."

Stride felt his back almost literally bending under the weight of it all. He dipped his head so his nose briefly brushed the top of Stonehide's head and then straightened up.

"And what about . . ." He nodded at the shattered tree trunk.

"I hear her voice," Stonehide said. "I see her in the butterflies. I get a little . . ." He looked down at the pile of splinters around his paws.

"I understand," said Stride. "It seems we have a lot in common. If I could hurt Death for taking Flicker from me, I would, Code or no Code."

"Don't say that," said Stonehide. "It didn't bring me peace. It didn't bring her back. All it changed was me. And I don't think for the better."

14

"*This is your last chance, you* know," Whisper said to Quake before they split up. Quake wanted to go back to the herd, not to find Bellow and Thunder, and that was fine by her. But she didn't much like the idea of sending him off to say Spirit-knew-what to Holler. . . .

"What do you mean?" Quake grumbled.

"Holler might try to kill Echo again. He might decide to do all sorts of things to hold on to power. This is your last chance to side with the Spirit and the herd over your father. Stand up to him."

Quake frowned. "My father wants only what's best for the herd," he muttered. "You're wasting your time going back to that broken-horned old fool."

"We'll see," Whisper said.

She watched as Quake headed off toward the herd, before she looked to Echo.

Her little brother seemed older as he met her eyes and said, "Where is Bellow?"

Echo hadn't grown any taller in the few awful days he'd been missing, but he was skinnier, and there was a look in his eyes that was far from the innocent, annoying little calf he'd been before he was chosen by the oxpeckers. She hated to think what he had been through in the custody of the lions. How scared he must have been.

But perhaps it was just exhaustion.

"I left him with Thunder," she said. "They're waiting for me. They didn't believe you were alive, so they probably think I've died too, looking for you."

Echo's expression brightened a little. "Then let's go and surprise them!"

It was another daunting journey across the plains toward the place Whisper had last seen the two adult buffalo, but now she had Echo with her. With every step she was alert for predators, but instead of only being poised to flee, she felt herself bracing for a fight. She had to get Echo to Bellow. There was nothing more important, her own life included. She hadn't come this far only to fail.

And although she scented hyenas, they found the meerkat burrows without much trouble, and the buffalo trail was right there, waiting for them. The closer they drew, the fresher the scents became, the more Whisper's heart raced. Echo trotted along dutifully at her side, barely talking. She had hardly had a chance to stop and tell Echo how much she missed him, how glad she was he was all right, but when they found Bellow there would be a little time to rest and celebrate. . . .

At last, the large dark shapes of two grown buffalo came into sight, resting beneath a tree. Whisper nudged Echo affectionately as they walked up to the tree and then called out, "Thunder! Bellow! It's us!"

Both buffalo looked up, and Thunder got to her hooves and clattered over to them, eyes wide with amazement. "By the Spirit! It is them! Echo, my baby . . ." Thunder nuzzled her nose against Echo's, and he gave a happy little grunt. "Whisper, I'm sorry, I should have come with you. But Bellow . . ." She sighed and squeezed her eyes closed for a moment, lowered her voice so that both of them had to lean in to hear her. "My dears, I so am glad you made it back to us now. Bellow is dying."

"*Dying?*" Echo gasped. "It's that bad?"

"He can't stand up any longer," Thunder murmured. "His wound is infected, and he has a fever. I don't know how much longer he can last."

"Then I need to talk to him now." Echo said. "Right?" He looked to Whisper, who nodded.

"I don't know exactly how this works," she said, "But yes, let's go."

The three of them hurried over to Bellow's spot beneath the tree. The old leader lifted his head slowly and gave them an exhausted smile. Whisper could smell the infection in his wound and tried to control the twitching of her nose and ears—it smelled like death.

"Echo," Bellow groaned. "I am so happy to see you." He leaned over with a pained grunt and touched his unbroken horn to Echo's horn buds. "Your sister is very brave. And she loves you very much. She never gave up, even when we all thought you were dead."

Echo scuffed the ground with his hooves, but he looked pleased too.

"What do we do now?" Whisper asked. "Do we . . . we can't get you both to the ravine," she said, hesitating for just a moment before deciding that there was simply not time to pretend everything was fine. "Can you still give Echo the wisdom of the migration?"

Bellow let out a long sigh. "We should wait for dawn at least," he said. "I am . . . afraid I may not make it that far. I can feel my grip on this world slipping away."

"No," Echo gasped. "It can't be too late! Do it now, whatever it is. I have to save the herd. . . ." Whisper saw a wild light in his eyes.

He needs this. We all need this. There must be something we can do. . . .

"The light fades," Bellow said. Whisper looked up, but it was still morning—and then she realized that Bellow wasn't talking about the sun. His eyes looked milky all of a sudden, and Whisper's heart skipped a beat. "Come, Echo. Come closer."

Echo knelt down, between Bellow's huge front hooves, and leaned his head close to Bellow's nose. Whisper longed to hear what Bellow was saying, but she stepped back, knowing this was for Echo alone. She had never witnessed the passing of the wisdom from one buffalo to the next—few had—but she fancied she could feel something different in the air. Something special, and ancient, and mysterious.

Whisper watched from the corner of her eye, the huge buffalo and the small one with their heads bent together, for what felt like a long time. At last Echo looked up, and she gave him a hopeful stare. But when she saw that his eyes held a lost expression, she turned her attention to Bellow. It was then that she realized the old buffalo wasn't breathing. His spirit had flown, leaving only a great stillness.

"I think he's gone," Echo said.

Whisper and Thunder both knelt and bowed their heads. Whisper felt like she was the one who'd fallen in the river and was being swept away—she felt untethered to the earth for a moment, as if Bellow's presence was the only thing keeping them all with their hooves on the ground.

Thunder stood. "We must go soon, dears," she said. She didn't elaborate, but Whisper knew what she meant. The scent of death would attract predators. Already there were flies crawling across Bellow's hide. But soon would come the vultures, and the hyenas, and the painted wolves. And with Echo here, even a small clan of scavengers could spell big trouble.

Whisper looked at Echo and fought a brief, furious battle with herself. *I won't ask. It's not for me to know. He'll tell us if he needs to.*

But she lost.

"What did he tell you?" she asked.

Echo shook his head, his eyes wide and dark. "It—it didn't make any sense. I don't want to say until it makes sense." He frowned miserably, and Whisper wondered if he really believed that it *would* make sense or was simply trying to hope it would.

"All right," Whisper said. *Well. Bellow has passed . . . something on to Echo, and that means it's time to go back to the herd.* "Let's go," she said.

"Holler won't give up power easily," Thunder warned.

"But we won't give up either," Echo said. "Will we?"

Whisper's heart squeezed in her chest. "No. Never."

There was nothing left to do but return to the herd. Whisper, Echo, and Thunder all touched their noses to Bellow's unbroken horn one last time, and then they left him in the shady spot by the tree and followed the sounds and scents of the buffalo.

What will Quake have told them? Whisper wondered. *And what will Holler do about it?* There was no telling whether Echo could even help them without the proper rituals done. She resolved not to ask him again if he had any idea what Bellow had said, but it was still hard not to wonder.

It wasn't difficult to find the other buffalo. In fact, they'd hardly moved since earlier in the day. As they reached the outskirts of the herd, the grazing buffalo looked up and began to mutter among themselves as they passed by. Some of them called out to Echo, delighted that he was alive, celebrating his return as if the sun had come out after a long rain. Others stared in flat disbelief or even suspicion. Most of them followed after him, though, gathering in his wake to see what would happen when he found the knot of males who surrounded Holler.

When they did come across Holler and his favorites, it was Quake's voice Whisper heard first.

"There were *ten lions*," he was saying. "And when they turned on us, I thought none of us would make it out alive. But I said no, you can't do this, and I fought one off, but more were coming. . . ."

Echo looked up at Whisper with a confused frown, and she rolled her eyes.

"My hero," she said loudly.

Quake jumped.

"Tremble and Trudge were killed by the lions," she said. "And Bellow is dead too. He died of the wounds inflicted on him by his brother. We should all be mourning their sacrifices instead of telling tales of our own daring."

Several of the buffalo had the decency to bow their heads, despite everything.

"But Echo is alive," Whisper went on. "And he is our rightful leader."

Holler turned slowly and gazed down at Echo. Whisper could sense him gathering his thoughts, and she did not trust his thoughts one bit.

"Welcome back, Echo," he said with a deep bow. "I

apologize that I did not believe you could have survived that awful fall. It is a relief to have you back in the herd where you belong. Now we can move forward, together, on our true migration path."

He paused, staring down at Echo, his gaze intense.

Whisper's heart sank.

Echo doesn't have a true path to give us. He can't just take control of the herd if he doesn't know what Bellow's words meant.

Holler was betting on this, and he was right.

No buffalo could depose Holler by force. He was too strong. And the herd would prefer the safety of a strong leader to taking the steps to get rid of him, even though they *knew* he had lied, cheated, and attempted to kill his way to the top. As long as everything went on as normal, they would all pretend they never heard that he'd tried to have Echo killed.

The giant buffalo leaned down until his nose was close to Echo's and spoke in a voice Whisper had to bow her own head in to hear.

"I welcome you, and I welcome your guidance, little chosen one. But I lead this herd. If you have nothing to say, stay out of my way, and we will get along just fine. Understand me, calf?"

"Yes," said Echo.

"Good," said Holler, and with a look of smugness that made Whisper's blood boil, he raised his head and bellowed, "Herd, to me. We march!"

15

"*She doesn't get a vote!*" *Hidetearer* yowled. "You must be joking! She was exiled from the clan as Tailgrabber and comes back with a new name expecting everyone to forget the past."

"And it's not like Gutripper welcomed her back," said Ribsmasher. "She was already ailing and weak."

Breathstealer stayed quiet, her heart thumping in her chest. Out of the corner of her eye, she could see a faint white smudge in the dry grass, the nearly clean skeleton of her mother where they had dragged her out of scent-range of the baobab. The body had been picked apart overnight by vultures.

One night leaderless, and now it was time for the clan to choose their new matriarch—and it was not going smoothly. For a start, few hyenas could remember the last time there wasn't an old matriarch to defend her rule by combat. Gutripper had killed the last one, and she had killed the one before.

At last they had been about to have a vote, each hyena placing a bone at the feet of the hyena they believed should lead them. And then Nosebiter had come up to Breathstealer, a long white rib bone in her mouth, and instructed her to cast her vote.

They had been arguing about it for some time now.

"Don't be ridiculous," snapped Bloodlicker. "She came back to try to save Gutripper, despite being exiled. Which one of you would show such dedication?"

"And she was *right*," Nosebiter added. "No hyena could have guessed what happened to our mother. Breathstealer deserves a chance to come home."

After everything that had happened, somehow the fact that there were other hyenas willing to stand up for her alongside Nosebiter was one of the greatest shocks. The decision to exile her had seemed to be unanimous, but perhaps Gutripper's vote had counted for much more than the feelings of hyenas like Bloodlicker. Now that she was gone, views were bubbling to the surface that had clearly been lurking for some time. . . .

"What's more," said Legcruncher—an unexpected ally, whose mind seemed to have changed entirely since Gutripper's death—"this means she really is getting visions from the Great Devourer! She is the Great Devourer's chosen! Don't you want a hyena like that in the clan?"

Well . . . I'm either its chosen, or it's trying to kill me, Breathstealer thought. *I'm not sure anymore. . . . Maybe it's both. . . .*

Her mind kept flashing back to the sight of Gutripper's

fur crawling with scorpions, of them scattering and vanishing into the grass. She had never seen scorpions behave like that before.

Insects brought the future to me. Sent me here to try to prevent it. And then insects made it happen anyway.

What if . . .

She shook off the thought.

Unbelievably, Nosebiter was winning the argument.

"Does she even *want* to stay?" Hidetearer whined in a blatant last-gasp attempt to win, glaring at Breathstealer.

"Yes," Breathstealer said. She was quite surprised how clear the answer was in her mind. But despite it all, this was her *home*. The clan had been a frustrating place to live, but it was much better than nowhere at all. "I do."

"Then she gets a vote," said Nosebiter.

And enough of the clan were nodding that Hidetearer's head went down, hackles rising, and she snarled, "*Fine.*"

Breathstealer picked up the rib bone and held it proudly in her jaws, and then the voting began.

Chaos reigned for a moment as hyenas tried to vote for hyenas who were themselves crossing to vote for someone else. But after some nipping and growling, a few distinct piles were beginning to form. A little way away, the males stood and watched, unable to vote on who would lead them, and seeming to care only in a very distant way.

One of the piles was Nosebiter's. One belonged to Hidetearer, whose tail was thumping smugly beside it. There were others who had a scattering of votes, but already Nosebiter and her supporters were separating out her pile and counting them. Breathstealer knew she would vote for her sister too, but she didn't move yet, wondering just how close it would be.

Only a moment later, she regretted that choice. It was going to be *very close*.

She hurried over and put her bone in Nosebiter's collection, and then she backed away. But it didn't stop the murderous looks from Hidetearer and her supporters when the bones were counted, and Nosebiter came out the winner—by a single vote.

"Nosebiter!" the cry went up, loud from Nosebiter's supporters and reluctantly from most of the others. They all lined up and sat, raising their chins and waiting.

Breathstealer remembered this from her cubhood, when Gutripper had become leader. The clan would offer their throats to their new leader, showing their total loyalty. She had bared her tiny throat, and her mother had nipped playfully at it and made her laugh.

She lifted her chin as Nosebiter approached, uttering the words of leadership as she set her teeth at each of their throats: "I drink your blood."

"My blood is yours to drink," responded each hyena in turn.

"I drink your blood," said Nosebiter at Breathstealer's throat.

"My blood is yours to drink," she replied. And she meant it, more than ever. She was part of the clan again, and it was all down to her sister. She owed her everything.

Afterward, they brought out prey from the den where they

had stored some earlier. Nosebiter took the biggest and freshest piece for her own, and while the others squabbled over the rest, as was only right, she began to call hyenas to her. Selecting her favorites, her council, as any matriarch should.

Some of them were ones Breathstealer knew Gutripper had trusted; others Nosebiter had made her friends. Some were a surprise. An elderly hyena named Pawbreaker, who Breathstealer had half thought was dead, hobbled over and regarded Nosebiter with a shrewd glare. And Hidetearer was also there, in a move far subtler than Gutripper would have ever made.

"We need to talk about the lions," said Nosebiter. "Gutripper's strategy was good. Noblepride's numbers are few, and with few cubs left to fight for them in the future. And yet"—here she glanced at Breathstealer—"such an aggressive strategy cost us dearly too. We can afford to be more cautious. I will send a spy to see how many healthy adults they have left and how many cubs."

"I'll go," Breathstealer volunteered at once. *Let me go. I won't cause more trouble for no reason, and I need to prove my loyalty to the clan. . . .*

"Good," said Nosebiter. "Leave at once, and you might be able to return by nightfall. Now, I want to talk about *our* cubs. We've far too few. Legcruncher, go to the males and bring me a representative. One who can speak in full sentences, please."

The hyena council cackled, and with that the conversation moved on. Breathstealer rose, stole a last mouthful of prey from an almost-bare gazelle carcass nearby, and set off.

Her paws felt light, and the strange events of the past few days felt far away as she climbed the hill and crossed the plain, toward the black rock river where she had killed the lion who killed Nosebiter's cub and the territory of Noblepride. She was back where she belonged, and this time she would be listened to, taken seriously.

She did grieve her mother's death. But if she was totally honest, out here alone, between the dry ground and the relentless sun overhead, she grieved not being able to save her more than the loss itself. Nosebiter would be a better matriarch. Breathstealer would have a better life.

If only her mother had been able to see . . .

When she heard the hornets buzzing, she realized it had been on the edge of her hearing for a while, camouflaged among the sounds of the plain. Not every insect was a messenger. But there was something about the tone of the hornets' nest, when she finally spotted it low down in the branches of a bent tree, that made her heart race. She thought about turning and running away—she could outrun the swarm, and if it went for her, the pain would be unimaginable, even if she survived. . . .

But something kept her from running, even as the hornet swarm lifted from their nest and formed into a deeply unnatural column, like the tail of a whirlwind, twisting and swaying toward her through the air.

One day curiosity will kill me, she thought as she braced herself. *But I need to know what will happen!*

The drone of the hornets grew louder and deeper, blocking

out all other sounds. She began to smell the rotten scent of the bog, but she wasn't sure if it was really in the air or just in her memory. At last the voice came, doubly frightening for the fact she was out under the open sky, where any other creature could see what was going on.

"*Did I not reveal to you the future?*" the Great Devourer said. Its voice made the inside of her skull itch.

"You did," she said. "But I was too late."

"*Were you?*"

Breathstealer's pelt twitched. "Yes!" she howled. "I tried to stop it."

"*She would have lived if she had trusted you. But it was not in her nature.*"

Breathstealer flinched at the truth of the statement.

She took a deep breath. When would she have another chance to ask, flat out, the question that gnawed at her guts?

"Did you send the scorpions to kill her?"

"*It was her destiny,*" the Great Devourer replied.

"That's not a no," Breathstealer hissed.

"*Shall we bring her back?*" said the voice, and Breathstealer's chest hitched in shock.

"You can't," she said. "I've seen her bones. The insects and the vultures have done their work already."

"*Do you really think there is anything I cannot do?*" The hornets buzzed louder, closer. "*Do you think there is anything I could not do to help you if I wished?*"

Breathstealer swallowed. Winced. Her hesitation gave her away, she knew. Could the Devourer read her mind? Or could it simply see what was in front of its thousand eyes?

"I have shown you a better life. A fraction of the power I offer," the Devourer said. *"I can make it better still. Follow me, and find your confidence in flesh, if you still doubt in spirit."*

Breathstealer frowned, not understanding what it meant— but now the hornet swarm was moving away from her, away from its nest. It flowed and paused, drifted back, flowed on again. The deep vibrating drone grew fainter, but the feeling never quite left the inside of her head.

It wants me to follow. And I will, I know that I will.

She began to pad along after the swarm. It moved faster, and she was forced to break into a run. She knew she was being led toward Noblepride's territory, and she felt a deep unease as the scent of lions grew stronger and stronger. This was her plan all along, and yet she hated that she was hurtling headlong into their territory with barely any time to breathe, let alone take care not to be spotted. She was supposed to be *spying*. Was the Great Devourer going to get her killed after all?

Then she almost ran face-first into the hornet swarm as it suddenly stopped and swirled around her, forcing her back against a large rock.

"What was that?" snarled a low, lion-ish voice.

"I smell hyena," said another.

"Don't you hear the sound?" said the first.

". . . you're right. Could it be an ambush?"

"Here? Now? They'd be fools to try it."

"Fearsome, go and . . ."

But the lions on the other side of the rock never finished making their plans. With a buzz that almost felt loud enough to shake the earth, the hornet swarm flowed up and over the rock, and Breathstealer heard yelps, growls, and then cries of pain.

It's stinging the lions. It's driving them away.

She risked a cautious look around the side of the rock. The sight she saw was awful, and wonderful. Four lions, beset by stinging hornets, stumbling away from the carcasses of two huge, *huge* adult buffalo. The lions had been eating but had barely scratched the surface of the mountain of delicious-smelling meat.

The lions already had swelling stings blossoming on their faces and their backs. They were trying to run. Two of them couldn't seem to control their legs anymore, and they stumbled and fell, twitching in pain, before managing to clamber back onto their paws.

"The trees!" one of them managed to yowl. "Get to the trees!"

The lions did their best. It was a painful moment before at last all four of them had limped and scuttled over to the tree line and vanished into the undergrowth, their yelps of pain slowly fading into the distance.

The Great Devourer's voice spoke, a whisper in Breathstealer's mind, as the hornet swarm began to dissipate into the air. In a moment, it was as if they had never been there.

"The pride will not return to this place tonight. Bring your clan. Share this feast. Take what is due to you, my chosen champion."

At last, the buzzing in her skull ended, and Breathstealer was left alone, but for the few flies that crawled across the heap of buffalo hide. She stared at the meat, drool dripping from her jaws, and saw comfort, trust, *respect*. She saw a future for herself being carved ever deeper into the bones of the earth.

Is this what I turned down? Just because I felt something was . . . strange? It's all strange!

She *would* bring her clan. Whatever else she was or was not, she was a clan hyena once more, and she would do her duty.

16

"It is insects, usually," said Stonehide. "Mostly at dusk. I don't know why. I sense her presence, and . . ." He trailed off with a wistful sigh that was at odds with his normal gruff manner.

They were walking down the middle of a wide ravine, between dangling vines and the bent trunks of old trees. A trickle of a stream ran along beside them. They were quite close to the forest and the Great Mother's clearing now, they just needed to follow the long, shallow slope. The elephants must come this way too, fairly often from the telltale cracking of high-up branches and the enormous footprints beside the stream. Not to mention the thick scents from the great dung piles.

"Do you think she's . . . trying to tell you something?" Stride said. He almost didn't want to suggest it, in case it upset his friend. "I just have such a strong feeling that Flicker is trying to communicate with me."

"I don't know," Stonehide said. "I've never had dreams like yours. But I do wonder sometimes. If it's really her, I think she must be trying to tell me something. But . . . maybe just that she remembers me. That she remembers being alive. Something like that."

Stride stayed quiet, but his mind was spinning. He supposed it could just be a message of love, a stray spirit who kept finding its previous mate. There was always the possibility it might not be her at all, that Stronghide was seeing and hearing things, just because he longed to see Silvertail again.

But neither of those answers felt right to him. He had no doubt it was Silvertail. The coincidence was just too great. He felt as if the paws of the Great Spirit were on his back, lightly moving both him and Stonehide toward some common fate, like a mother helping her cubs to find a path across difficult ground.

But if Silvertail was really speaking to Stonehide, what was she trying to say . . . and why hadn't she been able to say it?

"Flicker spoke to me, in the dream . . . ," he began. He wanted to ask Stonehide if Silvertail ever said anything to him besides calling his name, but he never got that far, because a scattering of stones from up above him caught his attention. They rolled and bounced down between the trees, clattering on rocks and splashing into the stream. Stride looked up and saw a dark, lithe shape, rounded ears twitching, peering down at them.

It was a cheetah. And as it leaped, bounding down the

steep slope toward them, he realized it was Jinks himself. He remembered the last time he'd seen his enemy, as he and Flicker had fled. It had been a moment of sheer jubilation, ripe with promise. At least for them. Jinks had been mad with fury, shrieking curses as they fled together.

"Stonehide," Stride growled. "Watch out."

For a moment, Stride considered fleeing. He didn't want this fight. They might make it out of the ravine. . . .

But if Jinks wanted a fight, he would still catch up with them, and then Stride would be tired. Better to stand and face him now.

Jinks was looking skinny, and he had a cruel expression in his eyes. He'd never been the most pleasant cheetah on the plains, but he had always had a smug swagger about him. Not now. He seemed cloaked in shadow, his fur dull and matted in places. He leaped down in front of Stride with a dark snarl.

Stonehide made a chuckling noise and moved to get between them. Jinks looked down at the honey badger and then up at Stride.

"Using this little . . . *thing* to fight your battles, Stride?" he rasped. "Like you used Flicker?"

For a moment, Stride thought about letting Jinks find out just how this *thing* could fight. It would be all he deserved. But instead, he put a paw gently on Stonehide's flank and then stepped past him.

"If you're sure," Stonehide said under his breath. "I'm right here if you want me to break his ankles."

Stride faced Jinks.

"I heard you were hanging around this territory, hiding behind a honey badger," Jinks sneered.

"I heard you've been promising impressionable young cheetahs that you'll give them some kind of prize if they hobble me," he said. "Afraid to do your own dirty work? Or do you think you can't beat me?"

"Beat you? I pity you," Jinks spat. "You couldn't get your own female, so you stole mine from me. And now it seems you can't even keep her. Or have you hidden her away, afraid I'll come and take her back?"

Stride blinked.

"What do you mean?" he asked, a little stupidly, before Jinks's words sank in. The other cheetah's lip curled in disdain and distrust, but he wasn't making a terrible joke or trying to hurt him.

He didn't know.

"Flicker, come out!" shouted Jinks. "Come and see what I do to him!" The thick forest swallowed his words. "Where is she?" asked Jinks.

Stride didn't know how to answer. He'd just assumed Jinks knew. That *everyone* knew. But as he dwelled on it, he realized that there was no reason for news that had shattered his own world to have spread.

"No matter," continued Jinks. "I'll find her later and tell her what I did to you."

"Jinks . . . ," Stride muttered. "I thought you . . . Flicker died."

"What?" Jinks spat. "Don't be stupid."

"No, she . . . she is, she's dead," Stride said.

Jinks glared at him. A flinch of doubt crossed his face. "No games," he said. "You're a liar. You're trying to keep her from me, but it won't work."

"Friend," said Stonehide from the rock where he had sat down to watch this confrontation, "he's not lying to you. Flicker is dead. You could ask the Great Mother if you don't believe either of us. Her vultures tasted the death and deemed it good."

"She ran too fast, Jinks," Stride said. "There were lions, and . . . she ran, and then she died."

"No . . ." Jinks looked back at Stride, and Stride saw a strange reflection of his own feelings on the other's face. Grief and shock—twisted by Jinks's anger, and his delusional entitlement, into a rage that made every hair on his back stand on end. His jaw shook as he bared his teeth. "*You. You killed her!*"

Stride snarled at him, and Jinks snarled back, beginning to circle Stride, his tail swishing. Stride's claws pulled from their sheaths, and his ears twitched back, waiting for the strike.

"You didn't protect her. *I would have protected her!*" Jinks reared up, aiming a swipe at Stride's eyes. Stride bucked too, claws out, both of them up on their back legs for a moment. The air between them was ripped to shreds by claws that never quite met fur, and then Jinks twisted and launched himself at Stride, bowling him over on his back in the stream. Stride raked his claws over Jinks's side and brought his back legs up to kick furiously at him. He felt the satisfying *ooof* of breath leaving Jinks's lungs as his paws thumped into his belly, but then Jinks's teeth were in his shoulder, and he hung on even as he twitched and gasped for breath. Stride tried to kick again. But Jinks's teeth were in his flesh, and he felt it tearing, hot blood running down to join the water of the stream. He yelled out and dug his claws into the back of Jinks's neck, but tore out only a chunk of fur.

"I can jump in any time," said Stonehide dryly.

Not yet, thought Stride. With a great heave he managed to roll and twist, just enough to get one paw planted on the streambed. He shoved up, forcing Jinks's head to turn uncomfortably far, and the other cheetah finally let go. Stride didn't bother to pull away, but thrust his muzzle at Jinks and bit down hard on one leg. Jinks abruptly went tense.

I could break it. I could hobble him and see how he likes starving to death.

The face of his brother flashed before his eyes, and Stride hesitated. And then Jinks was on him again, raking his claws across his side. Stride yowled with pain and released the paw.

Stonehide . . . it might be time. . . .

He opened his mouth to call out Stonehide's name—and Jinks landed on his stomach with both front paws, knocking the wind out of him in a painful gasp. Stride's chest hitched and burned as he tried to get his breath, and Jinks stood over him, his eyes flashing with menace.

And then all of a sudden, a giant snake came out of nowhere and wrapped around his back legs, lifting him into the air. Except it wasn't a giant snake at all. Once Stride's vision had stopped pulsating from the lack of air, he realized it was a huge gray trunk. An elephant stood over them, black eyes glinting angrily. Jinks writhed and yowled in the air, tried to scratch at the trunk but couldn't reach.

"What are you doing?" the elephant said.

Was this the first time an elephant had ever snuck up on a creature? He hadn't heard or scented her coming, preoccupied with the pain. He glanced at Stonehide, who didn't look surprised at all, and guessed he had seen her coming. . . .

"Let go of me!" screamed Jinks. "I'm killing this, this, mate-stealing, murdering traitor!"

"Do you need to kill him to survive?" said a voice. More elephants were crowding the ravine, and among them was Starlight. She squeezed to the front, and the elephant who'd grabbed Jinks raised him even higher so that he could look into the Great Mother's eyes.

"Yes," said Jinks through bared teeth. "I'll die of *shame* if I don't."

"And you'll be a Codebreaker if you do. Is that the choice you would make, cheetah?"

"*Then so be it*," Jinks snarled.

Great Mother Starlight gave a great sigh and looked at the elephant who held him. "Take him far enough away that he can't become a Codebreaker tonight, please, Raindrop."

"No! Let me go!" Jinks went on screeching and hissing and clawing the air even as the elephant carried him, not too gently, back the way they had come. "I'll kill you, Stride," he yowled, fixing Stride with a last cold glare. "When there are no grass-eaters to protect you, I'll find you!"

Stride sat in the stream for a moment, getting his breath

back, letting the cool water wash over his wounds and listening as Jinks's voice grew quieter and finally vanished.

"That, I assume, was the cheetah Jinks," said Starlight gently. "Did you tell him Flicker was dead?"

Stride nodded.

"Then I hope that he finds peace soon," she said, with a solemn bow of her enormous head.

I don't think he will, Stride thought.

"And if he does not," Starlight went on, "I hope that you are ready for him. After all . . ." A wry smile lifted the corners of her mouth. "He is quite right, you will not always have us grass-eaters to come to your rescue."

Stride got up and bowed his head, feeling a sting of embarrassment, somewhere below the hot ache in his shoulder.

"Come with us, both of you, and tell me what happened with the buffalo calf," Starlight said, and the elephants began to move, treading carefully to allow Stride and Stonehide to walk alongside. Stride started to tell the story, but then he let Stonehide take it up, falling silent as Jinks's words echoed in his head. Not just his threats, but his accusations.

Is it my fault Flicker is gone? Is it my fault she's still in trouble?

17

"*What are we going to do?*" Echo said. "I want to help, but I don't know how!"

It had been days since Whisper and Echo had returned, and despite setting off with a new confidence, the herd had immediately run into trouble. The remaining grasses were sparse and dry, hard to chew. Much of the ground was dust.

"We'll figure something out," Whisper replied. But she didn't know what to do any more than Echo did. Without Bellow's guidance, every buffalo in the herd could accept that Echo was the chosen leader, but it wouldn't help when they had no way of steering the herd right. And Holler might be a strong leader, but it was clear he had no idea where they should be going.

"I'm so hungry," Echo said quietly. Whisper's heart ached, as she could hear in his voice that he didn't want to complain out loud and upset the others. She wanted to reassure him, but the same hunger gnawed at her guts too. The longer it took to find the migration, the longer the hot season wore on. It burned grass, killed trees, and dried up watering holes. The predators seemed angrier, too. The herd had stopped moving at all in the heat of the day and had started traveling only at dawn and dusk, when the shadows were long and the temperature lower. Holler's one and only good idea so far. Still, the sight of the old and weak, too malnourished to move, was becoming more common. Vultures circled constantly, looking for anything dead or close enough not to put up a fight.

"We have to find good pasture soon," groaned Call, "or we'll starve before we find the migration path."

"If we don't find the path," retorted Clatter, "there won't be any good pasture left!"

"Well . . . ," said Call, and he looked at Echo. Echo shifted his hooves uncomfortably on the dry earth, and the oxpeckers that roosted on his back seemed to turn and look at Call and raise their twittering voices a little. Many of the little birds had gone back to their normal behavior, riding around on the herd's backs, eating the horseflies and other insects that were drawn to them. But there were still a big flock of them that wouldn't leave Echo alone. To Whisper, they almost sounded defensive.

They're right. He's doing his best.

"We need help," she said, stepping in front of her little brother. "We can't just carry on and hope that it'll sort itself out. Let's go back to the Great Mother. She sent that cheetah and the honey badger to help scare off the lions, and Brave-lands is relying on us. The Great Spirit will want to help, right?"

The other buffalo around her all nodded slowly.

"We should tell Holler," said Call. "Let's go."

Whisper hesitated before following him. Part of her wished they could just sneak off, but they couldn't afford to antago-nize Holler too much, since he seemed to have decided that outright murdering them wasn't worth his while. Or at least his grip on the herd wasn't strong enough that they'd let him get away with it. And in any case, Call was already moving. She hurried along with him, Echo at her heels. They picked up several stragglers along the way, including Thunder, who nudged Whisper comfortingly in the back of the neck as they walked.

Holler was surrounded, as always, by his strongest and most loyal favorites and several younger males who hoped to get into the inner circle one day—Quake and Stomp were hanging around on the edge of their circle, and they ran to warn Holler as they approached.

At least they were not hogging the good grass now—but then, all that meant was that there *was* no good grass.

Their tails were constantly swishing and their ears twitch-ing, and when Whisper drew closer she realized they were covered in horseflies, and there wasn't a single oxpecker in sight. She glanced at the flock still perched resolutely along Echo's back and felt a sort of guilty smugness at the loyalty of the little birds.

The heat of Holler's dislike was obvious as he turned to face them. But this time she wasn't bringing bad news or anything controversial. Surely he would approve of them simply asking the Great Mother for help?

But she had underestimated his temper and his pettiness.

"Ask for *help*?" he growled. "How dare you? *I* am the leader of this herd!"

Whisper bristled and took a breath to object on Echo's behalf. But one of the males, Thump, whose face was a mass of horseflies, snapped, "If your runt of a brother can't find the way, perhaps he'd be better off back with the lions."

"Last time we tried to ask her Greatness for help, she was useless, and your friend—*your calf* was killed," snapped Rumble, with a glare at Thunder. "Why would we take that risk again?"

Whisper felt cold and glanced at Quake, then up at Thunder. Thunder's eyes were shadowed beneath her hair.

She could fight. She could insist that nobody forget it was Quake who led Murmur into the quicksand on purpose, knowing she would probably die. It felt like a betrayal of Murmur if she didn't bring it up again.

But there were bigger things at stake. Quake would never be punished, not while Holler was in charge—after all, Holler had given him the order.

So she took a deep breath and swallowed her protests. Instead, she said, "Great Mother Starlight is wise, and she has already helped us. We should try."

Holler gave a great, dismissive sniff. "I am so tired of

hearing of these *wise* elephants. Aren't *we* the most powerful creatures in Bravelands? What elephant would not fall
beneath the hooves of a buffalo stampede? We make the rains
come with the very pounding of our hooves!"

"But we haven't!" Whisper snapped. "Have we? The rains
haven't come, and we'll all die before they do unless we *do*
something!"

"Silence, impudent calf!" Holler bellowed. He tossed his
horns and stamped, uncomfortably close to her face, and even
his followers backed away a little. Whisper tried to stand her
ground, but she felt the thumping of his hooves resonating in
her chest. "No buffalo will go to that arrogant old creature
while I am the leader!"

"You're not the leader!" Whisper cried out, unable to stop
herself. "You're big and loud, and you can gore me on the spot
if you like, but you're not our leader, and you never will be!"

Holler snorted, hot breath stirring the hair on Whisper's
head, and then his horns had struck her shoulder—but he
pulled the blow, simply nudging her aside. She almost fell but
kept her hooves. His eyes were fixed on Echo, and he stomped
over to the calf and sneered at him.

"So you would have this babe lead the herd," he said. "Then
tell us, Echo." He cast his head around. "What should we do?
Tell us, oh wise one."

Echo was trembling. "I . . . I don't . . ."

Holler suddenly broke his gaze, blinking and tossing his
head again, and Whisper saw flies crawling up into one of
his ears. He snorted and shuffled and turned back to Echo

with a furious rumble. "*I, I, I don't . . . ,*" he mocked. He lowered his voice. "Make a decision, child. Make it good. Which way? We're all waiting for your great, *great* wisdom."

Echo took several steps back and closed his eyes. He looked like he was thinking, or maybe listening to some voice speaking to him that the others couldn't hear. . . . Whisper hoped so with all her heart.

"That way," he said in a faint voice, nodding toward the horizon.

"Then let's go," snarled Holler. "Why don't you call the herd? Make sure you do so loudly."

Whisper's heart sank. Why was Holler so *cruel*?

Echo coughed and raised his small muzzle to the sky. "Herd! To me!"

A few of the buffalo looked up. Some of them took a step toward him uncertainly. The vast majority of them didn't even notice. Echo sagged, his eyes shining with embarrassment.

"I don't think they heard you," said Holler. "Try again."

Echo drew a breath and repeated the command.

A couple of the males laughed.

"Why are you such a bully?" Whisper said quietly.

"Whisper," Thunder muttered. "Be *careful*!"

"Yes," said Holler in an undertone that seemed to shake the ground. "Be careful. I have been patient. I have been *forgiving*. But challenge me again, and I will forget that you are a calf."

Forget that the others are watching, more like, Whisper thought, looking up into Holler's furious eyes. *If you thought you could get away with it, you would have killed us both without a second thought days ago.*

"If you had shown allegiance to Echo when he was chosen," she said, "Bellow would have been able to pass on the secrets of the migration. The herd would be safe. Bravelands would be safe. And you know it."

"That's nonsense. Holler beat Bellow in a duel," sneered Stomp. The young male looked down his nose at her. "That's the ways of our ancestors. Not some little birds choosing our leader for us. If Echo wants to be leader . . . ," he sniggered, laughing in advance at his own joke, "let *him* challenge Holler to a duel!"

Holler's cold fury warmed a little, and he let out a barking laugh. The others around him laughed too, each one seeming to find the joke funnier and funnier. The buffalo with Whisper—Thunder and Clatter, who had gone quiet since her suggestions had been so roundly rejected by Holler—did not laugh. But Stomp looked smug, soaking in the approval of the bigger males. Whisper felt sick.

"All right," said Echo.

Whisper's head whipped around to look at her little brother. Was she hearing things? What was he thinking?

The males hadn't even noticed. But Thunder had, and so had Clatter.

"No, Echo," Thunder started to say. But Echo was taking a deep breath, filling his little lungs with air, and before Whisper could stop him, he shouted out:

"I challenge Holler for the leadership of this herd!"

They heard it that time. The laughter fell silent.

Whisper moved closer to her brother. She just wanted to usher him away before his words got him into trouble.

"Do you now?" said Holler. His tone was hungry. Murderous.

"He didn't mean it," interjected Whisper. "He's just playing around."

"I meant it," said Echo seriously. "And a challenge cannot be withdrawn, can it?"

"It cannot," said Holler.

"Under one condition," Echo added. He wasn't shouting now. He lowered his voice and let the others lean in to hear him, and Whisper would have been impressed if she hadn't felt so terrified for him. "I choose where we battle. The one who remains standing is the winner."

"This is preposterous," Thunder said. "Holler, you can't do this."

"You'll kill him!" cried Clatter.

Whisper saw in Holler's eyes the moment he decided to murder her brother for the second time. This was all he needed: the opportunity, the excuse.

"If you insist," he said with a solemn nod. "I respect your bravery, little one. Choose the spot. I will follow."

Echo gave a serious nod back. "Come with me," he said and started walking away, his head held high. Whisper watched in horror as one by one, the other buffalo began to follow after Echo, Holler hanging back with a smug smile.

Whisper rushed after her brother, catching up with him

and talking urgently under her breath. "Echo, *please*. He is going to kill you. You can't fight him."

"I know what I'm doing," Echo said. "I've got a plan."

"We can still get out of here. We can leave now and find the Great Mother, and she can—"

"No, Whisper." Her little brother looked up at her, his eyes wide. "He will never accept me, and the rest of the herd will always be too scared of him to stop listening to him unless I do this. Don't worry. I'll be all right."

"Please," Whisper said again. He sounded oddly calm, but he must be delusional.

Echo nudged her with his small horn nubs and then peeled away from her at a trot. She tried to follow, but at that moment several of Holler's thugs bustled her aside, separating her from her brother and making sure he could no longer hear her desperate entreaties. Through their legs, she saw Echo sniffing at the ground. Then he raised his head and looked back at Holler. "Here," he said in a surprisingly loud voice.

He had chosen an open space near where they had been trying to graze before Clatter decided to try to talk sense into Holler. It was a slight dip in the ground, surrounded by little clumps where bushy grasses had been growing before the buffalo arrived. Perfect for all the buffalo to gather around and watch as her brother was . . .

She shook her head, trying not to think it. She didn't want to watch. She'd seen her brother die once, in his sudden plummet from the cliffs. But this would be far worse. Holler would surely trample him to death or gore him, and it might not be a quick end.

Echo stood in the middle of the bowl and waited. Thunder came and stood beside her, her bulk doing a little to calm Whisper's thumping heart.

"What's he thinking?" asked Whisper, beside herself.

"I have no idea," replied the older female. "But I believe in him."

Whisper wished she could say the same, but as she turned around and saw that Holler was approaching, she couldn't escape the dread that weighed her down. He was three times the height of Echo, perhaps ten times the sheer mass. The herd was all gathering to witness the strange spectacle, and she listened to them chattering, all of them repeating the same shocked things—*he can't, this is ridiculous, what are they thinking?*

Holler walked down to join Echo. The sight of his massive bulk beside Echo's soft, babyish frame made Whisper's chest physically ache. She squeezed her eyes shut.

"Whisper," said a voice. She looked up and saw Quake standing at her side. She winced.

"Go away," she said through her teeth.

"I don't want this," Quake hissed. "I can't believe Father's going to do this, it's not fair!"

"It wasn't fair when he challenged Bellow, either," said Whisper. The two buffalo were circling now, Echo trotting to keep up with Holler's measured pace. "Your father's a coward, Quake."

"I know," Quake whispered. She looked into his eyes a

moment, and he added, "I'm sorry. For everything."

She didn't know what to say to that. Though she didn't doubt his sincerity, it wouldn't help Echo now.

The circling went on, unbearably slow, the two buffalo getting closer and then farther away. Holler seemed reluctant to charge first, and for a moment Whisper thought maybe, just maybe, he would discover a tiny spark of decency after all and call it off. . . .

But then Echo reared up, gave his best bellowing grunt, and lurched toward Holler. With a deep roar, Holler charged, full speed, toward the little calf. Echo's hooves seemed to falter, his speed slowing. Whisper's heart raced and her vision swam. Would Echo run? Would he be caught on those huge horns, tossed into the air and broken on the ground?

Holler's head went down, his hooves pounding on the dry ground, and then—

For a moment, Whisper couldn't tell what had happened. Holler had stumbled to a halt, a few hoofsteps from Echo. He wobbled. His legs seemed like they had a life of their own, like they were trying to escape from under him. He slipped, slid, and fell down on his side. And then Whisper realized what she was seeing.

He had charged right into the center of the bowl, and the ground had given way, hard earth turning to a deep bog, disguised by a layer of dry dirt. This empty bowl, surrounded by dead grasses, had been a watering hole until the long hot season. Great clots of thick mud exploded from the ground, spattering Holler and the closest of the spectators.

Whisper's racing heart beat harder, and a hysterical laugh bubbled up inside her. Echo hadn't trodden in the mud. Echo had waited until he was on one side and Holler was on the other before he baited the enormous buffalo into charging at him.

He had known all along.

Holler was writhing and groaning, trying to get up. Whisper twitched, reminded of Murmur's end in the quicksand, as his furious stomping made him sink even more—but the bog wasn't that deep, and he seemed to get stuck up to his chest in mud, glaring furiously up at Echo, who stood on the edge of the soft mud and looked down at Holler.

"Do you give up?" he asked.

"Stupid calf!" Holler sputtered. "Of course I don't give up! You didn't beat me!"

"Who's still standing?" said Echo.

Holler stared at him, and his snorting came harder and angrier as he realized his mistake. "Help me!" he roared, making another effort to stand. This time his hooves slid and he went face-first into the mud, coming up blinking and choking. Echo raised his head and looked around at the crowd of buffalo around the dry watering hole.

"*Who's still standing?*" he repeated at the top of his small voice.

"Echo," said a buffalo near Whisper.

"Echo!" cried Thunder.

One by one, the buffalo took up the call. Echo's name rebounded from the sides of the watering hole and startled birds from trees.

"Echo! Echo! Echo!"

"Echo!" Quake cried.

The sound almost drowned out Holler's cursing, but not quite. Thunder hurried down to Echo's side with several other adults, and they stood around Echo while a few of Holler's friends—Stomp, Rumble, and some others—made their way to the bog and gingerly started trying to pull and shove him up out of the mud. He complained as they did so, ashamed to need their help, but requiring it nonetheless.

At last, Holler was freed from the bog, and under the gaze of the rest of the herd, with Echo's name still resounding in the air, he glared at Echo, swaying. For a moment, Whisper feared he might still attack, but the sheer effort of escaping the mud had clearly exhausted him. He collapsed to his knees.

"He bows!" roared Thunder.

"He bows!" came the response.

The new chant went up, and if Holler wanted to protest, no one would have heard him anyway.

Whisper joined the raucous cry. It was going to be okay. Echo was leader now, *really* leader, and they could go to the Great Mother, and they would fix this. It could all be okay.

She tried to ignore the pinched, foreboding feeling in her guts when she looked at Holler's face and saw only violent hatred in his eyes.

18

In the clearing, the anthill rose above her, crawling with insects. It felt oddly cool in its shadow, and she shuddered.

"I've come to give thanks," Breathstealer said. She felt slightly foolish. She wasn't sure this would work—despite everything, she had never reached out to the Devourer like this. Perhaps she hadn't needed to find the anthill, swarming with tiny black bodies; perhaps it would hear her wherever she was. Perhaps she didn't even need to speak aloud. But it had seemed like a good idea anyway.

"The clan hasn't eaten like that in seasons. They send their thanks."

She had told her sister what happened, and Nosebiter had chosen to tell the clan that their bounty was thanks to the Great Devourer—and thanks to Breathstealer's gift, her link to the Spirit itself. Whether all the hyenas had been comfortable with the explanation was a moot point—they had feasted until their bellies groaned and no one was questioning Breathstealer's place any longer. Well, not openly.

In days, Breathstealer had gone from a nameless exile to a full member of the clan. There were still plenty of hyenas who didn't like her, but even Hidetearer had kept quiet about it while the taste of the two huge buffalo was still on their tongues. It was very good, and very strange.

As she contemplated her good fortune, she began to see patterns emerging in the movement of the ants. She wasn't sure at first whether they were just the strange march of an anthill, perhaps changing direction in response to having a hyena breathing down their necks—but now the little black bodies were pouring out of the anthill, gathering in bigger and bigger numbers on the surface, forming shifting pools of black against the bright, pale earth.

She heard a sound that she recognized instantly, the sound that was a deep vibration between her rib bones—the Great Devourer *was* here. The pools of ants contracted and pulled apart, and for a moment she saw two pale openings in the crawling blackness, and it looked as if a great creature had opened large, blind eyes in a huge black face.

"*No thanks is required,*" said the Devourer. "*This is a taste of the rewards to come, for you and your clan.*"

"I—I still don't quite understand," Breathstealer began. She swallowed back the name of the Great Spirit. She was sure there must be a way of setting that niggling worry aside without antagonizing this powerful force, ruining the new life she had just grasped for herself. "What did we do to deserve these great rewards?"

"*What you are is enough,*" came the reply. "*Once, all hyenas were our loyal servants, feared by all, walking side by side with death. It will be so again.*"

"*All* hyenas?" Breathstealer gave a nervous chuckle. "I mean, I can do my best, but half our clan still doesn't really trust me. A lot of them didn't want me back."

A subtle change in the blank expression of the ant-face: a narrowing of the empty eyes. A wave of anger, rippling in strange formations, that swept through Breathstealer herself as if it was her own rage.

"*You bring them miracles. The lions give up their prey to you. Their bellies ache with hunger, their cubs weaken and die in their mothers' wombs, while the clan feasts until they can barely walk. And they still do not trust you?*"

"Some of them," Breathstealer. "They don't really believe I'm speaking to you—or they're jealous, or they think it's . . ." She stopped herself. How could she tell the spirit of death that these days, some of its servants thought it was *weird*?

"*Challenge them!*" The voice of the Devourer echoed in her rib cage and made Breathstealer shudder. "*Drive them out! It is time. Call our name, and no disbelievers will remain.*"

"I will," Breathstealer said, feeling strengthened by the voice.

But could she really? She had only just been accepted back into the clan. Was it really time for *her* to be driving other hyenas out?

"*Do not doubt us,*" said the Great Devourer. "*Those who have made that mistake in the past have paid the price, food for our swarms.*"

Breathstealer pushed aside her worries, or rather they fell away as the ants suddenly seemed to wake up, realize they had clustered together in an unnatural pool, and scattered down cracks and into holes in the dry earth.

She was just climbing the slope, looking up at the top half of the baobab tree sticking up over the crest of the hill, when her nose twitched with a familiar scent.

Wolf. Graypelt?

She stopped, looked around her. At first she didn't see him, though her nose insisted he was here. And then, out from under a dry bush, she saw the lone wolf emerge, long silvery nose, two paws, skinny frame, and bushy tail.

"Graypelt!" she whispered, looking around to make sure they were alone and hurrying over to the wolf. "It's me! Breathstealer!"

"I knew it was you," said the wolf with a pleased canine grin. "You smell different from the others."

"I guess . . . maybe that hasn't worn off yet," Breathstealer said with a frown. She had been back with the clan now for as long as she had been apart from them. How long would the smell of exile linger on her?

"Did you save your mother?" Graypelt asked.

Breathstealer hesitated. "No," she said. "She believed me, but . . . not quite enough."

But was that it? Was there ever any way to save her? Wasn't

this just the clan's destiny?

Isn't this the Great Devourer's plan? And honestly, is that a bad thing?

"Things are . . . all right, though," she said, not quite wanting to admit to him that they were *better*. "My sister's taken over the clan, and she's a good leader. She's invited me back in. And we had some incredible good fortune. I am sad for my mother. But we're going to be all right. How about you?" she asked. "Have you been finding food?"

"Enough," said the lone wolf. "I think you should be careful, though, Breathstealer."

"Why?" she asked, her ears pricking.

"I smell something on you," Graypelt said. "Something . . . dark."

Breathstealer forced a laugh and waved his concern away with a flick of her tail—which of course he couldn't see. "Dark? Darker than just being a hyena, I suppose?"

"You misunderstand me." Graypelt stepped closer, lowering his voice. "This is not the scent of hyena. It is not the scent of death. The darkness I feel is not a simple closeness to death and killing. It is . . . hard to explain to a sighted creature. When I stand at the edge of a precipice, I can feel the emptiness in front of me. I can sense, to some small extent, when a creature means me harm because it hungers, or fears me, or because it is cruel. When I say I scent this on you, I am trying to describe it in words that you'll understand. Do you, Breathstealer? Do you understand?"

I do. I know exactly what you're getting at. You feel the Devourer's presence, and you fear it.

But why? Why would it be more frightening than death, worse than hunger? It is death, it's not cruel. It can't possibly have some ulterior motive. He's the one who doesn't understand!

Breathstealer swallowed. "You've lost me," she said with another forced chuckle. "But I'll bear it in mind. Listen, it's really good to see you! But you should probably move farther away, you're well within hyena territory here, and the others won't be kind if they catch you. I can't guarantee your safety."

Not yet, said a tiny voice in her head. *Maybe one day, there are some rules I will be able to change. . . .*

"Remember what I said," said Graypelt as he turned to slink away. "If you need my help, you will be able to find me."

"Thank you," Breathstealer said seriously, though inside she was thinking, *Why would I need you . . . ?*

"I don't like it," said a voice. "*Tailgrabber* has too much influence on this clan."

Breathstealer knew at once who it was. *Hidetearer.*

She couldn't see the other hyena, or the group of females with her, hidden around the other side of the massive trunk of the baobab tree. But she could hear their nervous laughter.

"She wanders off by herself all the time," said one hyena. "She *talks* to *insects*."

"Maybe one's crawled in her ear and is nibbling her brain," said Hidetearer to a chorus of laughter.

"She's a freak," said another hyena. "She's always been a freak. It's only because her sister's in charge that everyone's suddenly tolerating her."

"Nosebiter's soft too," said Hidetearer. "And she wouldn't even be leader if Tailgrabber had been rightfully barred from the vote."

"And she wouldn't have been able to vote if not for Nosey," said one of the others.

"It's a conspiracy," Hidetearer snarled. "They cheated, and now we're stuck with this creepy cub. We should make sure she meets with an accident before she gets her teeth any deeper in this clan."

"I don't know," said one quiet voice. Was it Ribsmasher? "She brought us the buffalo. I haven't been this well fed in a long time. . . ."

There was a sharp chorus of hissing, and the uncertain voice fell quiet.

"What kind of price are we going to pay for that buffalo, though?" muttered Hidetearer darkly.

Despite their insults and their jeers, that was what made Breathstealer's heart race with anger.

You, pay for the buffalo? I already paid for it!

She paced around the corner, her hackles raised. It was time to trust in the Great Devourer's guidance. He was right—she must embrace the connection, proudly and defiantly.

"Hello, Hidetearer," she said.

The group of hyenas jumped, and one of them yelped. Breathstealer snarled in satisfaction.

"Anything else to say?" Breathstealer said, standing over Hidetearer. The other hyena shuddered but then got to her paws, facing her muzzle-to-muzzle.

"Yes," she said. "I think you've forgotten your place."

"And what is *my place*?"

"With the males, scavenging for scraps," growled Hidetearer. "Or in the ground with the insects you love so much!"

Breathstealer regarded Hidetearer with a cold stare. This hyena thought she could dictate where Breathstealer went, and with who. Did she think Breathstealer was afraid?

"Do you know where I go when I go off alone?" she asked.

"To stick your nose in wasps' nests," said Hidetearer. "Like a freak."

"I speak to the Great Devourer itself," said Breathstealer. "I know you know this. Even if you don't believe it, why would you risk insulting the spirit of death itself?"

"Don't be ridiculous," snarled Hidetearer.

"Am I being ridiculous?" Breathstealer whispered. She took a deep breath. "*Great Devourer*," she said, tipping her head back, staring up at the sky through the leaves of the baobab tree. "You told me to call. I call you now. Show these disloyal hyenas why they shouldn't doubt me."

There was a pause. Hidetearer laughed, and the others began to join in nervously until their cackling echoed in the air, until suddenly one of the hyenas broke off with a startled yelp. Hidetearer's confident laughter broke off as she turned. Something huge and black was crawling across one of the hyena's faces, and she leaped up and shook her head madly, trying to dislodge it. It was a spider.

Breathstealer looked up and caught her breath. A swarm of spiders was dangling from the branches of the baobab, hundreds and hundreds of them, swaying on thin lines of silk. They hung over the group of hyenas like a cloud. Or a threat. The sight was majestic and terrible.

"The Great Devourer," whispered one cowering hyena.

Are they venomous? If I asked, would they kill Hidetearer, let her die in the same agony Gutripper did? She's a bully and an unbeliever. Does she deserve any better?

Hidetearer squirmed away, out from under the swarm, and glared up at the tree and at Breathstealer. "You don't belong here," she hissed. She was trying to show nothing but anger as she turned and scampered away. But she wasn't fooling anybody. Her darting eyes and her flattened ears screamed fear.

Breathstealer looked back at the rest. They were staring at her and up at the spiders, terror and awe in their eyes. She stood and took it in silently. Let them think twice before they talked about her like that again.

A spider spooled slowly down and landed, ever so gently, on her shoulder, and Breathstealer smiled.

19

"So," Stride said, "what do you think? I've got no reason to doubt he's really sensing the presence of his mate. But what does it mean? Could she be trying to tell us something?"

"Silvertail died a natural, if terrible, death," said Great Mother Starlight, frowning and curling her trunk from side to side. "Bravelands suffers daily a multitude of tragedies, but it is the way. A thousand small griefs are the price we pay for this life. Trust me, Stride, the Spirit feels them all."

Stride dwelled on her words. He'd never thought of it that way before. But it must be true, for the Great Spirit knew everything. He wondered, did it grieve too? How could its heart cope with all the suffering?

They were sitting in the forest space where they had last argued, and she'd given him the mission to find Echo. And little seemed to have changed.

"He seemed . . . possessed," said Stride. "But I don't think he's gone mad. In fact, he's quite normal at other times."

Starlight sighed, her brow furrowed. "If Silvertail has gone to the stars with the other spirits, I would not expect her to be able to come to him. Nor would I expect her to need or want to."

"That's what I thought," said Stride, his fur prickling with apprehension. He'd thought about telling Stonehide that he should come with him and explain to Starlight about his visions of Silvertail himself. But he had changed his mind when he'd realized that this way, he could voice his thoughts about it—and his fears—without forcing his friend to face what could be a difficult truth before he was sure. "Is it possible she might have been claimed by the Great Devourer? Could she be sending butterflies to him to try to warn him?"

Starlight hesitated. "More insects," she rumbled. Stride's ears pricked. What did she mean, *more* insects? "I fear it may be possible, but I simply cannot be certain, not yet. It might not be her at all."

For a moment, Stride thought she was doubting Stonehide's truthfulness or suggesting they were both imagining it—but her tone was so dark, he suddenly wondered if she meant something much, much worse.

"You mean . . . it could be a *trick*?" he gasped. "But why? Why Silvertail, why Stonehide? Why not communicate more clearly," he added, his mind spinning, "if it's some other thing trying to trick us?"

The Great Mother heaved another enormous sigh, her

huge shoulders rising and falling.

"I wish I had clearer answers," she said. "Many moves have been made to try to stop the Great Devourer's overreach. Your protection of the chosen calf is one of those moves, and it succeeded. When it comes to life and death, everything is connected. But many friends and allies have been tested, and some"—she shook her head—"some slip further away with every day."

Stride scratched at his ear, trying to follow her logic. He felt like through her dark eyes he could see her mind working, thoughts and ideas and plans blinking and changing like stars in the night sky.

He felt a sense of vertigo, looking into those eyes. There was so much happening. The fate of Bravelands, the balance of life and death.

It was too much. He didn't want to be involved in any of this, but he was, and for one very specific reason. He couldn't let himself forget it.

"I saved the buffalo," he said. "And I'm glad it was a success in your . . . your great *strategy*. But how can I save *Flicker*?"

"I believe that Flicker's spirit *can* be released," said Starlight. She was speaking slowly and carefully, and Stride felt like a cub being instructed in some basic life truth. "That if we can keep the Great Devourer in line, we can find a way to return the spirits to their rightful position in the stars. But Stride, you must accept that Flicker is dead. Even if we win her freedom, you likely will not see her again until you die, or . . ."

She stopped, blinked.

"What?" Stride pounced on her hesitation, like he would on unwary prey. "Or? Or what?"

"Stride," said Starlight seriously. "One thing I have learned is that there are places living animals should not go. Please, believe me. You would not save Flicker, you would only damn yourself."

"They say a cheetah stole the sun from the spirit of death," said Stride. "Did you know that? They say the Great Devourer had hidden the sun in its underground kingdom, and it was a cheetah who was fast enough to get there and bring it back."

"Some birds say the sun is the yolk of a giant egg," said the Great Mother dryly. "Some stories are just stories."

Stride bowed his head.

Maybe, he thought. *Maybe it's just a story. But the Devourer is real, Flicker's spirit is real, and Flicker's death—a sudden death after she ran too fast, just like the stories warn about—that was real too.*

So I suppose we'll see, won't we?

20

Echo's triumph sent waves of emotion through the herd. Exhilaration, relief, burgeoning hope—and deep anger, resentment, unease. Whisper could tell which were running high among the buffalo near her by the way they chattered excitedly or closed off when they saw her coming. Sometimes several emotions would pass over a single buffalo's face. As a herd, they'd been through such a period of uncertainty that now no one seemed to know what to think. It didn't help that the migration was still a stop-start affair.

The center of the herd had shifted, the pull of Echo's victory surrounding him with loyal—or perhaps ambitious—followers, mostly older females who ensured that when he made decisions, they were heard loud and clear by every buffalo. Whisper was reminded of the time when he'd first been chosen, when suddenly he'd become extremely popular—except that back then, she'd been concerned he wouldn't need her anymore. Now he stuck close to her whenever he could, and he always seemed to need to know where she was.

She, on the other hand, was keeping track of Holler.

The old leader's followers clustered closer around him than ever, keeping a little separate from the rest of the herd. Whisper saw them muttering to one another, giving Echo furious looks, though they fell silent whenever they thought she could hear them. Holler himself, his head bowed, seemed to say nothing, but anger radiated from him, rising like the heat haze where horseflies still buzzed. Quake, meanwhile, seemed to vacillate between standing with his father and standing with the others, as if he could keep the herd together just by his presence in both groups.

"We should go to the Great Mother," she said to Echo, the morning after the duel. "You fought for leadership of the herd, so we could get her advice. We should go."

"You're right—I should send someone," Echo said. "A few of the big adult buffalo so that they're not in so much danger."

Whisper hesitated. "I . . . I think you might need to go. Starlight might want to talk to you directly. As the chosen leader."

She almost added, *And you need someone you can trust.*

"I suppose . . ." Echo frowned. "But I think the herd needs me, though."

Whisper shifted her hooves nervously. He was safer surrounded by loyal buffalo—but what if not all the buffalo were loyal? What would happen if Holler decided to attack? If they tried to get him from the middle of the herd, would the herd tear itself apart with fighting? What if one of the females who surrounded Echo was secretly on Holler's side? What if they managed to get him alone in the middle of the night . . .

Whisper shook herself. She wanted to protect her brother, but she needed help. Who could she really count on if things became desperate?

"They're not going to need you," she said. "You still don't have the wisdom of the way from Bellow, so you need to see the Great Mother, or you'll be no use to the herd at all!"

Echo frowned. Hurt and annoyance creased his small face. "That's not true! I am useful! You're always telling me what to do—I do know what I'm doing sometimes, you know!"

"Of course," Whisper said. "That's not what I'm trying to—"

"Echo," said a breathless voice, and Clatter hurried up beside them. "Lions. Scented on the edge of the herd. They smell hungry."

Echo's eyes went wide, his little ears twitched, but he took a deep breath and called out as loud as he could, "Form the Shell!"

"Form the Shell!" Clatter repeated. "Elderly and calves, to the center!"

The other buffalo took up the call, and the herd began to move, dust rising as their hooves struck the dry ground. Whisper looked around and saw tawny shapes darting between the large bodies, much closer than they should be. She turned, searching for the ordered lines, for her place within them—and Echo was gone. Where had he gone? Panic flooded her, and she gave an involuntary yelp. Had he gone to the front of the Shell? She tried to shoulder her way through, but stamping hooves and snorting muzzles blocked her path.

"Where are the lines?"

"What is happening?"

All around her, she felt chaos building. She heard buffalo calling out for one another, saw them rushing forward and then, instead of crowding together, falling back.

The Shell was failing. Why was it failing? *Where is Echo?*

She slipped between two large buffalo and saw a line half-formed, trying to stay between the calves and the lions, but it was as if there weren't enough buffalo to finish the Shell. . . . She spun on the spot, peering through dust and buffalo hair, disoriented by the scents of frightened buffalo and the far-too-close stink of lions. . . .

Where was Holler? Where were his followers? Why weren't they in the front, as the biggest buffalo keeping the herd safe?

"Get away! There's nothing here for you!"

That was Echo's voice. Whisper wheeled around, and she spotted him by the cloud of shrieking oxpeckers who were circling in the air over his head.

He was out on the wobbling, failing outer Shell line. He was trying to be the leader.

She began to gallop toward him. She saw a pale lion shape, bones standing out in sagging skin, turn, open its mouth in a roar, and make for Echo. Other buffalo saw it and tried to get to him, but the herd was chaos and the line moved too slow. Whisper put her head down and charged with a scream of terror.

Her small horns met flesh. She shoved and heard a yowl. The lion fell back, scrambling and hissing, baring its terrible teeth.

"Go!" yelled Whisper, shoving Echo. "Get back!"

The lion circled away, but not far, and then it was coming back, claws out, drool dribbling from its jaws. . . .

"No!" Thunder led a group of buffalo over, and the lion saw them coming, thought better of her choice, and turned tail.

"Thank you!" Whisper gasped, but Thunder nudged her.

"There are more," she said. "Holler's abandoned us, the Shell has failed. Both of you get out of here! Head for the gorge, we'll cover you." She tossed her head over her shoulder, and Whisper knew where she was pointing—toward a small gorge where they had found water that morning, water still bubbling from somewhere deep below where the baking sun couldn't stop it.

"Come on." She nudged Echo again. He hesitated, looking on, his face twisted with indecision as the other buffalo tried to form up between him and the lions. "Echo! If you die, we're all done for, come on!"

Echo's gaze fell back on her. He nodded. They ran.

Whisper could see no lions ahead, only confused and shifting buffalo. If they were lucky, the lions wouldn't manage to follow. If they were lucky, they wouldn't have circled the whole herd just yet.

They burst from the edge of the herd to confused and

distressed shouts from some of the other buffalo and encouraging shouts from others. There were no lions. There was just open ground, a small stand of trees and bushes, and on the other side the faint sight of rocks and glint of water.

Whisper almost tripped several times, looking back, sniffing the air, trying to make it impossible for any predator to catch them unawares. She could smell only buffalo, but the wind was against them. Any lion who wanted to could follow them and, if they weren't paying attention, sneak up on them.

I hope Thunder's getting everyone under control, she thought desperately. *I hope the calves and the elderly are all right. . . .*

"Let's go up," she said, looking up at the rocky gorge.

"Up onto the rocks?" Echo gasped, panting, his hair falling over his eyes. A few oxpeckers that had managed to keep up with them fluttered around his head.

"We'll be able to see any lion that comes near from up there," she said. "If we can make it over the boulders."

The oxpeckers started to tweet and call, and they flew over to the edge of the stream. They hopped onto the rocks, pecked at them, hopped to the next.

"Follow them," Whisper urged him. "It's okay. I'm right behind you."

They ended up climbing side by side, Echo's shorter legs needing guidance from the oxpeckers, Whisper managing mostly by herself. She stopped to check behind them about halfway up and saw buffalo coming toward them and no sign of the lions, and her heart swelled with relief—

And then Echo gave a yelp and fell back, his hooves clattering on the rocks. The oxpeckers lifted and cheeped around him as he scrambled, tried to catch himself, but slipped and tumbled clumsily backward. Whisper cried out his name as he hit the stream and rolled.

Her heart skipped a beat as she looked down, seeing him lying in a wet heap at the bottom. But he was breathing, trying to get up. And the buffalo were coming. It would be okay. She tried to turn to go down after him, but down was harder than up.

Slow, careful! It won't help if I break my legs, she told herself. She watched the group of buffalo approaching and took a breath to call out to them, but then she realized that they were larger, and closer, than she'd thought. Their horns were large, sharp and curled, and the hard boss across their foreheads joined together in the middle. And one massive buffalo emerged from them, standing over Echo's struggling form, horseflies swarming around his head, making him look like he was carrying his own angry cloud with him.

"What a pathetic creature," Holler snorted. He raised a hoof, pawing at the air over Echo's head. "You were never strong enough to lead."

Echo wobbled to his feet. "You failed to form the Shell," he retorted.

"Leave him alone!" cried Whisper.

Holler looked up at her dispassionately, before addressing himself to Echo.

"I didn't even hear the Shell call. Like I said, you're no leader."

"I bested you!"

Whisper was surprised at the vehemence in her little brother's voice.

"You tricked me."

"Being a leader is about using your brains, not your brawn," said Echo.

"Is it now?" said Holler. "And how are your big brains going to get you out of this place?"

"Escort me back to the herd at once," said Echo. "Move aside."

Holler peered over his shoulder at his accomplices. No one moved. Whisper saw that no one else was coming. They were alone.

"This game has gone on long enough," said Holler. "It's time for you to meet your inevitable fate."

"No!" Whisper yelled, and she jumped down the last few rocks, landing with a stagger and a splash. She tried to throw herself between them, but Rumble got in front of her first and shouldered her aside hard so she stumbled and fell. Other males closed in, circling her and keeping her from Echo, in a terrible mockery of the Shell that they had abandoned. She rammed them as hard as she could in the knees and the ribs, but though they stamped and yelled in pain and annoyance, they were too big to move.

"Be still," Holler snarled. Whisper could just see Echo between the legs of her captors. Holler put his head down and rammed him—head-on, not yet spearing him on the curled points of his horns, but knocking him flat once more. "I'll make this quick," he said.

"Murderer!" screamed Whisper. "Codebreaker! The herd isn't stupid, they'll all know it was you!"

"I'm sure they will," said Holler with a dark chuckle. "But do you think they'll care? If you two aren't there stirring things up, how long do you think it will take for them to fall in line?"

He reared up, his hooves kicking the air.

"No!" shouted a voice, and a hairy shape shoved between Holler and Echo. Holler's balance was thrown off, and he stamped down, one hoof cutting across the muzzle of the interloper. Echo managed to roll away, pulling himself up onto a rock behind the buffalo who'd put himself in harm's way.

It was Quake.

"What do you think you're doing?" Holler snapped.

"Enough!" bellowed Quake. "Father, enough! I won't let you do this!"

"*You?*" Holler sneered. "*You* would stand in my way?"

Quake's whole body was shaking. His eyes were mad with fear, and blood dripped down from the cut his father's hooves had scored across his nose. But he didn't move.

"You've done enough damage," he said again, his voice trembling. "I thought the herd needed a strong leader. I did everything you said because I thought that. But you're not strong. You're just a murderer. And you made me a murderer too!"

Holler's jaw was slack, staring in disbelief at his son. Whisper felt the males around her shuffle their hooves, amazed at what they were seeing, and she took her chance, aiming her horns for a gap between their legs and shouldering her way through and out. She clattered over to Echo's side and helped him up onto higher ground again, casting frightened looks back at Holler and Quake. The bigger buffalo wouldn't be able to follow them up here . . . she thought. She hoped.

Holler glared at Quake and up at them. "Kill them," he said.

Rumble moved first up the slope but staggered back as the ground broke under his weight. Several others tried to advance but couldn't get much farther. Quake picked a route up to just below Whisper and Echo, almost falling himself but managing to find purchase.

"You're making a terrible mistake," Holler growled at his son.

"It's not the first," replied Quake sadly. "At least I chose this one."

"How long do you think you three will last?" asked Holler. "A day perhaps? You'll see each other's bellies ripped open by flesh-eaters before too long."

"We'll take our chances," said Echo.

For a moment, Whisper wondered if Holler would make a last charge himself, but instead he backed off, turned with heavy hoofsteps, and began to walk away. The rest of his followers stared up at them in hatred and confusion, and then they trailed after their leader.

Quake stood, legs shaking, watching them go. Then he turned and started to climb up after Whisper and Echo.

They made it to the top of the rocks, and Whisper nuzzled

Echo and checked him for injuries while they waited for Quake to catch up.

"Nothing broken," Echo said. "Some—ow!—some bad bruises, like right there. Not as bad as Quake," he added as the young male finally clambered up next to them. His nose was still bleeding, thick oozing blood that Quake licked at, and then he winced in pain.

"What's happening in the herd?" Whisper asked. "What about the lions?"

"I'm not sure," Quake said. "Thunder's trying her best. The lions'll give up eventually. But I saw Holler heading off after you, and I didn't wait to make sure."

"What now?" Whisper asked. "Do we go back?"

"We go to the Great Mother," said Echo. He looked up at Whisper. "You were right. Sort of. We can't bring the herd together until we find the migration path."

"I'll come with you," said Quake.

Whisper stared at him. The sight of his face still made her hackles rise. She had spent so long hating him. She might never forgive him for his part in Murmur's death. He had been so *cruel*. Had all that been Holler's influence?

But he had spilled blood for Echo. It was still dribbling down and dripping onto the ground at her hooves. It had to be worth something.

"Then let's go," she said.

21

Breathstealer heard yipping laughter echoing in the darkness, and it sounded like home. She padded out across the dark plain, unafraid, knowing her kin were out there. She could hear them feasting, the sound of crunching, snapping, tearing, and cackling. She scented blood, lions, buffalo, and fear. And at last, the moon emerged from behind a cloud, and she saw what the group of hyenas had gathered around: the twisted, pale shape of a lion, with a thick mane matted with blood.

"Is that . . . ," she said, approaching.

"It's Noble!" cackled Ribsmasher, through a mouth full of dripping flesh. "Noble himself!"

"Guess there's no more Noblepride," giggled Legcruncher. "We won."

"Just a shame we didn't finish them off ourselves," said Nosebiter's voice. Breathstealer peered over the heap of stained fur and saw her sister look up, blood blackening her muzzle. "It smells like there was some kind of battle with the buffalo. Seems like it was messy. Something definitely got dragged away over there, and poor old Noble here got crushed."

"Poor Noble," echoed Ribsmasher sarcastically.

"Come," said Nosebiter. "Eat. We survive."

"We survive!" chorused the other hyenas.

Breathstealer came closer, finding herself a spot between Nosebiter and Ribsmasher, and stuck her muzzle into the thick fur, looking for a tasty mouthful. But she hesitated before she bit down. The flesh in front of her nose was moving. Crawling creatures flowed up out of the corpse over her nose, obscuring her vision. Breathstealer fought and won against the urge to flinch. She shut her eyes, letting the insects—flies, from the buzzing, but it was too dark to see—cover her whole face.

Show me, she thought. *Show me your truth. I'm here.*

She felt a great pressure, as if her head were being squeezed, as if the insects had suddenly become impossibly heavy. She tried to keep her nerve, but a muffled yelp escaped her throat as she was dragged headfirst into a blacker darkness. She heard her own blood thumping in her ears, rhythmical and strange. And gradually the thumping changed, the sound twisting, until it was a word. A name. *Her* name.

Breathstealer! Breathstealer! Breathstealer!

She was standing on a high rock, looking down on Brave-lands. She could see it all, places she had never been, places she could never see from a single vantage point; it was all some-how laid out at her feet. All around the rock, the largest hyena clan she had ever seen was chanting her name, yipping and snarling it hysterically.

She felt the presence of the Great Devourer at her shoulder, looking through her eyes, as the crowd of hyenas parted and a great gray shape came limping through. It was an elephant, huge and elderly, with eyes that contained a terrible sadness. She climbed the rock with awful slowness, lay down before Breathstealer, and tipped back her head to expose her throat.

"My blood is yours to drink," the elephant whispered. Breathstealer took a step forward, lowering her teeth to the creature's throat.

"Hurry up, Breathstealer," said Nosebiter's voice. "Or all the good meat'll be gone."

The pressure in Breathstealer's head lifted, so suddenly she felt dizzy and light, as if she might float away. The flies were taking off. She blinked, the moonlight blinding after the darkness of her vision.

She looked around, wondering if the others had seen the flies. They didn't show any sign that they had. She took a bite of lion meat and sat back to chew it, still feeling dizzy, and not just from the sudden ending of her vision.

Why had they all been chanting her name? Had she won some great victory? Had she defeated an *elephant*?

It sounded almost like she'd been made clan leader. . . .

But was this the future or some kind of message? And why would an elephant lie down and offer its throat to her?

She glanced over at Nosebiter. She wouldn't tell her sister about this vision, or if she did she might leave out the part about the chanting. She didn't want or need to be clan leader. Not while Nosebiter was making such good choices.

She left the rest of the clan to finish off Noble and headed off alone. She could almost hear the voices still—*Breathstealer, Breathstealer...*

Or perhaps it was just the thumping of her pulse in the quiet of the night....

"Breathstealer!" came a voice, a real, whispered voice. She jumped, but she recognized the voice at once.

"Graypelt? Are you still here? Where are you?"

She saw the wolf step out from the shadow of a bush, his gray fur catching the moonlight and seeming to shimmer with silver. How did this solitary creature keep finding her? It was uncanny.

"Come with me, Breathstealer," said the wolf, and ducked back into the bushes. Breathstealer frowned. She couldn't work out why he was still lingering—but he was surely testing fate, because the other hyenas wouldn't waste a moment wringing his life away if they came across another scavenger on their territory. She followed him through the undergrowth to a small clearing between a few twisted trees. The moon shone down through the shifting canopy, casting a strange mottled light down on them both.

"What do you want?" she asked. "I keep telling you, it's dangerous here!"

"It is," said Graypelt. "But not for me. It's yourself that you should be worried about."

Breathstealer's head tilted in confusion. "I don't understand.

I'm fine. I'm really good, actually."

"You are on a path that leads only to bad places," said Graypelt. "I have tried to be subtle, my friend. You have been kind to me, kinder than almost any of your kin would be, and I hoped that would mean you could resist temptation. But now I need to be clear."

"Well, I wish you would start being clear," Breathstealer muttered, although she suspected she could guess what he was about to say.

Sure enough: "The Great Devourer's intentions are not good," he said. "It will use you for its own ends. Remember your hesitation in the jungle. You knew it then. Do not go any further down this path."

Breathstealer took a deep breath. She thought of the jungle. Of her fear that something was wrong here.

And then she shook her head.

"Graypelt, I'm very grateful for your help in the bog," she said. "But you don't know what you're talking about. You're just afraid of the Great Devourer because it's a spirit of death. But death is natural, and it has done nothing but help us. I won't just give that up on the word of a blind wolf who doesn't understand our ways."

"Sometimes the blind see things most clearly. I know the ways of death," said Graypelt, lowering his voice. "I am a wolf, and I am telling you, it is a path that will lead you only to violence and loss. A wretched future for yourself and all of Bravelands."

"And I am a hyena," said Breathstealer, drawing herself up.

She was starting to get tired of the wolf's interference. After all, she had more than repaid the debt she owed. "I know violence. I know loss. And really, I don't care about the rest of Bravelands. They look down on us—all of them."

"You sound like *him*," said the wolf quietly.

The meaning of Graypelt's words was not lost on her, but they only stoked her anger.

"The Great Devourer is offering me something *else*, *finally*. Go away, Graypelt. I don't need your concern. This is my destiny, and you can take it from my jaws when I'm dead."

Graypelt sighed.

"If that is your decision," he whispered.

A twig crunched behind Breathstealer, and she twitched and spun around.

"Breathstealer? Are you in here?"

It was Nosebiter. When Breathstealer looked back around, the blind wolf was gone.

"I'm here," she said.

Her sister pushed through the bushes. Her head was cocked, and her mane stood up high on her neck.

"Talking to yourself?" she asked. "Or . . ."

"The Great Devourer," said Breathstealer simply.

Nosebiter stopped, took a breath. She regarded her sister with a calm but searching stare.

"I defend you to the others, your . . . visions," Nosebiter said slowly. "But it's really true, isn't it? You hear it speak? You . . . *command* it? I heard about Hidetearer and the spiders," she said, and even under the dappled moonlight, Breathstealer saw a slight grin cross her sister's face.

"I don't command it," Breathstealer said. "It shows me things. And yes, it speaks to me. I am the Great Devourer's chosen. Through me, we can be its loyal servants again, and in return . . . well, you saw the buffalo. And Noble, out there. All the miracles we can eat."

Nosebiter gave a tiny shudder, but she nodded. "Tell me what you hear, what you see. I will be guided by the Devourer through you." Then she stepped close to Breathstealer and headbutted her hard in the chest, knocking the breath from her for a moment. "But you will always be my little sister. First and always."

"Obviously," Breathstealer chuckled, gasping. "And with the Great Devourer watching over us, we won't need to worry about anything from now on."

EPILOGUE

Great Mother Starlight sat in the center of the dark Great Parent clearing, looking up at the stars. At her side, Raindrop shifted and used her trunk to scratch behind her ear. The air was still, but clouds were moving high up, scudding across the stars.

"My mother used to say that each star was the spirit of an animal," Starlight said. "And one day, so many spirits would have lived and died in Bravelands that the night would be as bright as day."

Raindrop's ears twitched. "There's a long way to go," she said.

Starlight smiled faintly. "Sometimes stories are just stories. Sometimes . . . sometimes a story is a path to follow. It doesn't matter if every creature describes the path a little differently— you can still follow the path to the same destination."

Raindrop looked at her, a frown creasing her wrinkled gray skin.

"You lost me, I'm afraid, Great Mother."

"Ah, well. Ignore me, child. Sometimes I'm just a rambling old elephant."

There was a shuffle in the branches of the trees, a rustle of leaves. Starlight looked up and saw a familiar shape hanging from a tree, the bright orange ruff around his neck glowing faintly in the moonlight.

"Excuse us, Raindrop," said Starlight.

"Of course." Raindrop got up and bowed to Starlight, and also to the flying fox. She left the clearing. Starlight and the flying fox waited in companionable silence until they could no longer hear the creaking and snapping of the undergrowth as Raindrop passed through it.

"I hope you have good news for me, my dear friend," Starlight said.

"I wish I could say so." The flying fox dropped from the branch and landed in the dry leaves on the ground. For a moment, shifting shadows played across it, so that Starlight couldn't see its proper shape.

Then the gray wolf stepped out of the shadow of the tree and came to sit beside her. He lay down, his muzzle resting on his paws, his ears flat with sadness.

"I have failed you, Great Mother. I have failed us all. I should never have left the hyena alone."

"Not your fault, Graypelt," said Starlight gently. "She was with her clan—there was little you could do to reach her there."

"She was so close," said Graypelt, letting out a long sigh. "She would have been a powerful ally. Now . . ."

Starlight laid her trunk gently on the top of his head.

"We will not lose hope, Graypelt," she said. "Breathstealer's loss hurts, but it is not our last gasp yet. The fate of Bravelands is finely balanced, indeed."

"Our enemies are multiplying," said the wolf darkly. "The Great Devourer grows more powerful all the time. And the buffalo are *still* in disarray. There will be so many, Great Mother. If it doesn't rain—at this point, if it *does*. Whether by fire or flood, the Great Devourer will feast on all those spirits if we don't do something."

"Something will be done," said Starlight. She looked up at the stars again, but the sky was dark, the stars almost completely hidden by the clouds. Only a few small, bright points could now be seen, winking down at them.

"The elephants are the strongest animals in Bravelands," Graypelt said, looking up at her, a little flicker of hope in his voice. "If it comes to battle . . ."

"I am not convinced that physical strength will win this war," said Starlight. "It will take faith. Loyalty. Courage, and sacrifice. It will take love."

"It will take a miracle," said Graypelt, dropping his head back onto his paws.

"Then let us be glad that miracles are all around us, old friend," said the Great Mother.